DOMINIC'S CLOSET
ADVENTURES IN OCULUS

Theresa Maria Villarreal

ISBN: 9798846593220

DEDICATION

This story is dedicated to my children, who inspired me to write this story. To my mother, who always supported me, and my mother-in-law, thank you for always believing in me. My children, your support means the most. I love you.

ACKNOWLEDGMENTS

To my husband, Ruben, thank you for editing my book. Thank you for constantly pushing me to do better and be better. You always believed in me, even when I didn't believe in myself.

1 THE DOORWAY TO AN ADVENTURE

Dominic was a boy like no other, with a rather fantastic imagination. He and his trusty dog, Leonard, had many adventures together. They always liked putting out fires, fighting aliens, or chasing dragons. They were loyal friends and went everywhere together.

Dominic always wore his black All-Star High Tops and his favorite lightweight red sweater, grey t-shirt, and pants. Leonard had a green collar that jingled so loudly that it could be heard from a mile away. Like most eleven-year-old boys, his room was filled with Legos and crafts to take on his adventures. Like many older brothers, he had a curious sister who wanted to join the fun. Dominic's sister, Rebecca, would enter everything in her brother's room. She was especially interested in Dominic's Lego collection. The best part of having a faithful watchdog like Leonard was that he kept Dominic's Legos safe from his sister. However, since Dominic and Rebecca were the only siblings in the house, they usually got along well. Dominic recently received a wardrobe from his mother, who told him to take good care of it as it is an important family heirloom.

One day, Dominic was in his room playing with his Legos when Rebecca came bounding in.

"No! Rebecca, you can't play with my things!" said Dominic. "Mom! Rebecca is touching my things!" he yelled.

While his sister was busy messing with his things, his mom entered his room. "Dominic, what's wrong?" she asked.

"Mom, she is in my room again," he said, pointing at his sister.

"You're going to have to get along with her. She's your only sister, and your job as her big brother is to take care of her," said his mom. She looked at Rebecca. "Rebecca, you must ask before entering your brother's room."

"Yes, Mom," Rebecca said. "I wanted to play with him. I have not seen him all day! He's been playing with Leonard."

"Dominic, since you are the oldest, you'll have to set a good example and play with your sister. I'll be leaving soon to go to work. Your Aunt Cori will be here to watch over you," said their mom.

As soon as his mom left, Leonard padded into the room. He licked Rebecca.

"Leonard! Yuck! Don't lick me!" Rebecca ran out of her brother's room and yelled for her mom down the hall.

"Good job, Leonard," said Dominic. "Way to keep the pesky beast away." He laughed.

Dominic and Leonard continued playing in his room, building a grand Lego castle together. They had designed the court with intricate towers and a grand archway, which Dominic called the "portal to another world." Leonard barked in agreement, wagging his tail excitedly. Dominic noticed his wardrobe door was slightly ajar as they finished their masterpiece. He couldn't remember leaving it open. Curiosity was piqued, and he walked over to close the door but saw something unusual as he approached.

A faint, humming sound filled the air, and Dominic could see what appeared to be a shining, spinning black hole on the back of his closet door. Bewildered, he leaned in closer to examine the strange phenomenon. Then, he heard barking coming from the other side of the portal.

Dominic entered the wardrobe, and Leonard was gone! "Mom!" he screamed. "Mom, Leonard is gone!"

Aunt Cori rushed into his room. "Dominic, you scared me!" Aunt Cori said. "Oh, thank heavens! I was worried you got hurt."

"Where is my mom?" asked Dominic.

"She left for work and won't be back until later tonight," said Aunt Cori.

"I can't find Leonard. He disappeared, and I'm worried I lost him."

"Dominic, don't worry; he's probably outside," she sighed.

Dominic could still hear a slight humming as she left the room. He turned to face his wardrobe. The black hole he had seen was more prominent and was spinning at a faster pace. Dominic peered into it. Then he heard barking.

"Leonard is that you?" he asked. The barking got louder as he stepped closer to the door. Without thinking, Dominic jumped into the shining hole in his wardrobe. Once he was through the spinning hole, the hole closed off. He had entered a new world.

Dominic fell until he hit the ground. As he got to his feet, he heard barking. Leonard came running to him, wagging his tail. He looked around and saw Leonard.

"Leonard!"

Dominic said. "Pup, you scared me. I thought I lost you. Don't do that again. You always need to stay by my side."

Leonard put his ears down low but still wagged his tail.

"Oh, pup, I'm not mad. I was worried," he said.

All of a sudden, they heard a low crack! Dominic and Leonard both turned. His eyes were wide with surprise. To his shock, he realized there was ice and snow. Around him were ice-covered hills. The hills are dotted with dozens of tiny, thatched-roof houses covered in snow. He saw smoke coming from the chimney stacks.

"Leonard, I don't know where we are, but I see houses in those hills." He pointed toward the hills.

They began walking in the direction of the houses. It was snowing softly and growing dark. Dominic and Leonard could only see their footprints in the snow and the light from the houses. Dominic realized they had found a small village as they got closer to their homes.

"Hey pup, it's quiet here. Do you think there's anyone around?" Dominic said to Leonard.

As Dominic and Leonard moved further into the village, Leonard began to bark. Dominic shivered. He did not have a winter coat. His teeth began to chatter, and Leonard continued to bark. Dominic was trying to silence Leonard when he heard the crunch of snow coming from behind him. A white figure appeared. It was a giant white yeti! The size of the creature's hands was astounding! The Yeti had white fur over its body, large yellow teeth, and gaping eyes.

"Run!" he told Leonard.

"Wait, don't leave!" said the creature gruffly. "I can help you. Let's head to my home to have a good talk."

Dominic was hesitant until the creature bent down to pet Leonard. Leonard yelped and sniffed and licked the beast. Dominic followed the beast. They journeyed through snow and ice until they came to the Yeti's home, which was a cave. Inside, Dominic found the shelter to be quite comfortable. It was well-lit, clean, and dry. It had a carpet on the floor, paintings on the walls, and a roaring fire. The Yeti had a table set for tea. Leonard lay down in front of the fire. The Yeti talked, and Dominic listened.

"Young man," said the Yeti. "Let me introduce myself. My name is Barnabus Barlow. I'm sorry I frightened you, but it's common for a yeti to appear big and rough. Don't let my appearance fool you."

"Sir, where am I?" asked Dominic

"This land is called Oculus," Barnabus spoke as he looked down at his hands. Dominic looked puzzled and asked, "Sir, why is this place so dark and cold?" "One day, darkness came to land in the form of a witch," Barnabus said. "There was a bloody battle between the guardians of peace, the Spider Witch, and her Spider Army. The Spider Witch ensured the king and queen were no longer an obstacle. She took their little princess Rebecca as her prisoner." The yeti looked down at the ground sadly.

"Rebecca is the sole survivor of the Spider Witch's attack on the royal family."

"That's awful!" Dominic was sad to hear this.

"It gets even worse." He looked at Dominic. "I was the family's chief advisor, and we had been trying to rid the land of the Spider Witch and her followers. My fault is that the king, the queen, and Princess Rebecca were

4

betrayed. I trusted too many people, which led to the downfall of the monarchy."

"We have to rescue her!" Dominic exclaimed.

"Many have tried and failed," said Barnabus. "They did not know how to get past the mermaids or the Spider Witch." Barnabus sighed. "We require someone who can bring hope." The Yeti sat quietly for a moment, deep in thought. He looked up at Dominic. "You may be the person from an old prophecy who promised. The prophecy said A little boy and a furry companion would come to save us all."

"Why do you think I'm that person?" Dominic was curious.

Barnabus stared at Dominic. "You are here to fulfill a purpose. Chosen one or not, will you help?"

"I think so," Dominic replied bravely. "But first, will you tell me more about the journey ahead?"

"Are they good or bad?" asked Dominic.

Barnabus was quiet for a moment and began with a story about mermaids who lived in Oculus.

"When the battle with the Spider Witch began, the mermaids neither chose the Spider Witch's side nor aided the king. The mermaids began aiding the witch when the Spider Witch won and took control of Oculus." They live at the bottom of the Black Lagoon.

"Why are the mermaids now working for the witch?"

Barnabus was matter-of-fact. "Mermaids are creatures who only help themselves. They only decided to help the Spider Witch because she gained all the power in Oculus."

Dominic was quiet, thinking for a minute. "How are we going to get past the mermaids? Once we do, how will we win against the Spider Witch?"

"An old friend of mine can help provide us safe passage and help us defeat the Spider Witch."

"How do you know it will work this time?" asked Dominic.

"I have gathered new information from rebels who want to help restore order to our land. The way to get past the mermaids is with the aid of a mighty staff," said Barnabus. "Where would we find a staff?" Dominic asked.

Barnabus didn't answer. Instead, he got up and opened a drawer that had tablecloths inside. Suddenly, Barnabus threw out the tablecloths and popped the bottom of the drawer. Then he pulled out a stick with a jewel inside it. It looked like a staff.

Dominic asked, "What is that?"

"This is my Jawa Staff. I am a Wizard, and a wizard must be above a staff, right?"

"What does it do?" asked Dominic

" The Jawa Staff is designed to protect against dark magic and the evil creatures that work for her." He placed the staff inside a large green canvas bag like a backpack.

Then Barnabus gathered more items for their journey. He took some things from the tea he set out earlier and placed them in sacks and bundles. Dominic got up to help Barnabus. They gathered up sleeping bags and blankets for their journey.

Before they left, Barnabus bundled Dominic up for the journey to the Spider Witch's castle. Then Barnabus opened the door to start their dangerous journey.

"It's important not to make sudden movements and not make noise as we travel through the land. The Spider Witch controls Oculus, and she gets reports on any activity. We don't want her to know we are coming. We want to keep the element of surprise,"

Barnabus said hurriedly. "Now, young sir, we'll meet up with an old friend on the way and cross to the other side of Oculus together."

They began their long journey in the cold world of Oculus. They could see dark water up ahead. Come to think of it. Everything was dark. Dominic wondered if everything had turned dark when the Spider Witch took over. He knew better than to ask or make any noise at all.

2 BUCKLE BOOTS, THE BRAVE

As they continued toward Barnabus' mysterious friend, Dominic noticed
Barnabus' large yeti feet walking in the snow. He also noticed how alert
Barnabas and Leonard were. As they walked, Dominic listened to the
rhythmic crunch of snow beneath their feet as snow continued to fall.

Dominic couldn't help but wonder if he had what it took to help save
the princess. His mind wandered, contemplating their quest and his role as
they trudged through the snow for many long, silent hours. Then he
noticed his surroundings were changing. He no longer heard the crunch,
crunch, crunch of the snow, nor did he see Barnabus' large footprints
anymore. Then Dominic realized how the seasons seemed to change
quickly the further they walked. Maybe there were different worlds in
Oculus, and the seasons changed as they passed into a new one.

Suddenly, Barnabus and Leonard stopped walking. Cautiously, Dominic,
Leonard, and Barnabus approached what looked like the shore of a lagoon.

"Is this the mermaid lagoon?" Dominic asked.

"No, this is one of many lagoons in Oculus," Barnabus answered. "You will know the mermaid lagoon because the waters are black. These waters are blue."

Barnabus led them down a sandy path towards a dock as they neared the shore. Dominic and Leonard then saw a marvelous sight. Dominic's heart skipped a beat. He looked at a massive ship with a flag hanging on the mainmast. The flag was black with a white skull and crossbones. A man walked down the plank of the boat and came towards them. Barnabus began walking to the man.

Dominic wondered if this was the friend Barnabus mentioned before.

The man spoke to Barnabus.

"So, sir, will you be joining me on the ship? Let us talk and share a meal. All of us, including this young sir and his pup," the man said with a smirk.

Barnabus smiled and nodded. "Of course, we require a good meal."

They followed the man to the ship and went aboard. The mysterious man led the way down the narrow stairs below deck. Barnabus, Dominic, and Leonard followed. Once Dominic and Leonard got below, Dominic met with a large round wooden table, a carpet on the floor, and a roaring fire. Gold plates, forks, spoons, and knives sat on the table. The table contained rich foods like baked ham, cheese, oranges, and bread. Dominic looked up at the man. He was tall with green eyes, dark curly hair tied back into a neat ponytail, a smiling face, and a scruffy beard. Buckle Boots had a dark blue buttoned-down shirt, a loose-fitting blue velvet coat with gold buttons, dark blue breeches, and long black boots. He had a gold loop earring and gold in his teeth.

The man gave a comprehensive look at Dominic as if he knew him but quickly composed himself in a light-hearted manner.

"Young sir, you must be hungry," the man said to Dominic.

"Why don't you make yourself a plate of food? You must be starving. Then we'll talk."

The man looked at Dominic and Leonard and said, "Oh, hey, little pup, let me get a plate of something for you."

He filled a plate with meat and cheese and set it down for Leonard.

8

"Now, Barnabus," said the man, "what is your plan?"

Barnabus leaned in and spoke urgently, "This boy, Dominic, is the chosen one we've been waiting for—destined to defeat the dreaded Spider Witch.

"So, you say. Now, boy, where are you from, and what brings you to our land?" asked the man.

Dominic noticed the man was direct but very kind to him, like a father asking questions to his son.

Dominic enjoyed his food but paused his eating, "I'll tell you if you tell me who you are and if we can trust you."

The man laughed. "I like him already, Barnabus. I shall tell you my name. I'm Buckle Boots the Brave, but you can call me Buckle Boots. What are ye called?" "I'm Dominic, and this is my faithful companion, Leonard. I'm from a different world. I came through a strange portal in my closet. Now, why are we here, Barnabus?" asked Dominic. "We are here for the company, and Buckle Boots has a gift for me," Barnabus said. "Now Barnabus," said Buckle Boots, "she'll be expecting you to bring that book and an army."

Buckle Boots put his thumb to his lips and looked thoughtfully.

"This is true, but she didn't know I would be a changed man and be working for the royal family this time." Then he laughed a great big pirate har, har, har.

"Yes," Barnabus laughed with him. "I have another mission for you soon," he told Buckle Boots. "I'll need you to move your ship eastward to the jungle of Oculus. Now, we have to be on our way early in the morning. Goodnight, for now, Buckle Boots." "Thank you for the meal," said Dominic as he finished his last bite.

"Yes," said Buckle Boots, "Good night and good luck, lads."

Dominic was taken downstairs to sleep in the captain's cabin by the captain's first mate Jamie.

Dominic got settled down for the night with his dog Leonard. Oddly, Leonard seemed more at home here than he had before. He acted almost like he had been in this place before and somehow knew Buckle Boots.

Dominic tried to get comfortable at night but kept shifting in the makeshift hammock. He finally found a suitable sleeping position; he felt someone was watching him. As he got up suddenly, he saw the light, then a figure heading back towards the stairs. He saw the outline of the Constitution.

"Buckle Boots?" said Dominic, wondering why Buckle Boots was watching him.

The next day, Buckle Boots gave Barnabus and Dominic much-needed supplies and a lantern to pass through the mermaid lagoon the following day. As they began walking, it was still dark outside, but Barnabus' face was well-lit. Dominic thought it was from the lantern, but the wick couldn't burn. As Barnabus got closer, Dominic realized the light had come from a book Barnabus was trying to hide. Barnabus saw Dominic peering at what he had in his hands.

He said quietly, "We better get to a safer place so I can tell you more about this book." The rain started pouring down as they made their way through the forest. Dominic, Barnabus, and Leonard had to find shelter quickly. Leonard barked and ran forward. Dominic and Barnabus followed. Leonard had led them to a cave. Barnabus went first to make sure it was safe. He beckoned Dominic and Leonard to enter, and they all sat down as Barnabus built a fire.

"Why did we meet with your friend?" Dominic asked.

Barnabus smiled at Dominic,

"He gave me a book that I thought was lost.

"I once told you I was the royal advisor and had to leave all knowledge and wisdom behind when the Spider Witch defeated the royal family. Now," he smiled again, "Buckle Boots has found one important element of Oculus' history that weakens the Spider Witch's hold on the people of Oculus." He whispered, "The Book of Knowledge."

3 A FRIEND OF BARNABUS

Barnabus, Dominic, and Leonard sat on the cave floor, well-hidden for many of the Spider Witch's spies. Barnabus' Jawa Staff lay beside him as he searched his rucksack or backpack. He pulled out supplies that Buckle Boots gave them before they left.

He put Dominic to work on making a meal as he looked through the Book of Knowledge. Leonard lay asleep next to the fire as Dominic cooked a stew pot. "The only sound heard was the crackling from the fire and the pages turning in the book Barnabus was reading.

Dominic stirred the pot and stopped, putting the spoon aside to let the soup simmer. Dominic sat back and stared into the fire. He started to drift off into a deep sleep.

"Dominic!"

"Sorry, Barnabus, I think I must have been more tired than I thought," said Dominic.

"Not to worry, Lad."

Dominic looked up to see it was not Barnabus but a different person across from him.

Dominic, puzzled, asked, "Who are you?"

"A friend of Barnabus, and might I say, you are still asleep."

"Then who are you?" asked Dominic.

The man wore a dark blue tunic with golden buttons resembling suns. His hair was wild and long if running through a forest. "He was not an older man, having a youthful face and a long brown beard, which was also wildly unkempt. His eyes were light brown, kind, and shining brightly.

"I am called Mrryden Wilt, but I think you would better know me as Merlin."

"You mean from the story of King Arthur?" asked Dominic.

Merlin paused and said, "Oh yes, from your world, and I am sure you have heard of the tale of Camelot, but you know the myth is from this very place."

"What do you mean?"

Didn't you know that a passage once connected your world to this one?"

"Oh," said Dominic, pausing.

"Oh, that is all you have to say?" asked Merlin.

"Well, I still don't quite understand why I am here or how we are talking together right now," said Dominic.

"You can only see what I want you to see and what your roots will allow you to see," said Merlin.

Dominic wondered what Merlin meant but didn't press him on this.

"So, why would you want to show me?" asked Dominic.

"I find you are critical to this quest, and I see my old friend Barnabus has found the Book that he and I made," said Merlin.

"Wait, you and he made this book?" asked Dominic.

Merlin nodded.

"But why?"

"This book is essential, as it acts as a fail-safe from enemies of Oculus, but can only be opened by one who created the book. By one who is part of this world," said Merlin.

"How does it work?" asked Dominic.

"When both someone who made the book and someone from this world uses the book together, the light will shine brightly, guiding all those who are lost back home," said Merlin, his eyes twinkling."

"Do you mean you and Barnabus must open the book together?" asked Dominic.

Merlin nodded.

"And, if you don't mind me asking," said Dominic, "Why, if you are alive, haven't you and Barnabus worked to defeat the Spider Witch, and where are you now?"

Merlin looked elsewhere, and his eyes had a faraway look.

"There was a battle," said Merlin.

He paused and closed his eyes.

"I was on the battlefield leading the free people of Oculus. We fought for days against the Spider Witch and her army. It wasn't a battle fought on a remote plain or a field but in the very heart of Oculus. Men weren't the only causalities. The battle, so bloody that it included whole villages, families, women, and children, left me unable to face anyone. I wandered for days and found myself in the woods outside the capital. I magicked myself into a home near the oldest Willow Tree of Oculus. I looked out and saw it was too late to intervene, and I returned to the woods."

Dominic stared and processed everything Merlin told him.

"You mean you abandoned the princess and all the people?"

"Not abandoned," Merlin said.

"Have you heard of the expression, He who runs away will live to fight another day?"

"No, but whatever the expression, you left people to a fate worse than death, and now you and Barnabus want me to save this land. I thought you were an 'All Powerful' wizard, and if you say Barnabus is the book's co-author, then why not the two of you go and defeat the Spider Witch?"

"You are the savior, and because of that, people like me and I are helping to bring peace and defeat the Spider Witch."

Dominic thought about this and said, "How are you helping?"

"You met Buckle Boots?"

"Yes, but Buckle Boots works with Barnabus," said Dominic.

"Who do you think told Barnabus to meet Buckle Boots?"

"So, Barnabus is a magician like you?"

"I trained him," said Merlin.

"I see," said Dominic," Is that why he knew about me and is quickly trying to get me to the Spider Witch, but the real question is why?"

Merlin paused and let Dominic think about this. He thought about what Merlin said but looked at the shadows on the cave walls that moved back and forth from the fire. The only sounds were the crackling fire and the gravel shifting.

"You and Barnabus believe I am the boy from the prophecy."

"What must I do?"

"Now, you are thinking like one from this land."

"First, you must get Barnabus to meet me by the high wall of the Spider Witch's Castle. He will be told there is a disturbance, but he must get to the wall as it is of the utmost importance. He will know why."

"Second, you both must have safe passage across the lagoon. You will meet a mermaid who will take you to the Mermaid Queen."

Merlin got closer to Dominic and said, "You must do exactly what she asks you to do."

"Once you get to the Spider Witch's Castle, you will meet another of my apprentices. She will guide you safely through the tunnels to get inside the castle undetected."

"Once inside, you will undergo several tests, and Barnabus will help you. However, as part of your journey, you will get separated. Whatever you do, always run. Don't stop and continue onward. The quest depends on you."

"Do you have any questions?"

"Yes," said Dominic.

"Well, what is it," said Merlin impatiently.

"How do you know all of this?"

"You know the future, don't you?" asked Dominic.

"That is your question?" asked Merlin, annoyed.

"Yes," said Dominic cheekily.

Merlin closed his eyes and massaged his temples, and sighed.

"Yes, but I believe you already know that."

"What is your real question?"

"What do I need to expect with the Spider Witch?" asked Dominic.

"What has Barnabus told you?" asked Merlin.

Dominic put his hand to his chin and thought for a moment and looked down and looked at his friend Leonard, still asleep. He then looked up and said,

"He told me that at one time, she was a beautiful lady from a land that is now gone, called Gehenna. He said this was a horrible place, and the people and animals were beyond help."

Merlin nodded and asked Dominic to continue.

"He said the Spider Witch was once so beautiful but desired power above all things, and an evil sorcerer had seduced her into learning about the dark forces that she wanted so much power and status and to rule everything, so she used dark magic and this dark magic, somehow caused her to be transformed into the figure she is today."

"And what else did he tell you, as I know my friend loves to tell how she got here and why she is here?"

Dominic was about to speak but paused, annoyed at how Merlin talked about his friend, Barnabus.

"I don't think I will, as you seem to know all, and maybe you can tell me,"

Said, Dominic.

Merlin realized what Dominic meant but decided not to apologize for his behavior, as why should he? He is a great Wizard, and they are trying to eliminate evil. He looked back at Dominic as Dominic asked another question.

"Why didn't she help her world?" asked Dominic.

"She craved power more than saving her world," said Merlin.

"Before coming here, she sent spies, tradesmen, and merchants that were her allies from other lands to come and find out if there was a weakness in Oculus."

"Well, did she?" asked Dominic.

"Yes, she did," said Merlin.

"You see, a magnificent king and his family ruled Oculus, and Oculus itself was created thousands of years before by the Son King. A great Wizard trained other wizards, but he had not been seen for many years, so the people grew to think they were better than what the land of Oculus and the Son King had given them."

"So, how does that create a weakness?" asked Dominic.

"They grew lazy even though they had a very wealthy kingdom. They relied less on each other and more on what they individually wanted."

Dominic still looked puzzled but continued listening.

"When the Spider Witch sent her army to conquer the capital, the people did not listen to the King's warning about finding refuge in our western lands but thought our army would easily defeat the Spider Witch's army, so the people unwisely stayed. The Spider Witch attacked and exiled rebel forces but put the people under a mind control curse after executing the King and Queen."

"So, what will she expect me to do?"

"She is very good at wagers, and she is very prideful."

"What? I still don't understand."

"Think!" exclaimed Merlin.

Merlin sighed impatiently.

"You like games, right?"

"Yes, but who doesn't?" asked Dominic.

He paused, then looked up at Merlin.

"Oh, I see," said Dominic, "you're saying I need to trick her into playing one to stall her, so I can pull the book out and open the fail-safe."

"Exactly," said Merlin, "I think I will leave you so you can tell Barnabus about our plans."

"Wait," said Dominic.

"What part of the wall does Barnabus need to meet you, and where exactly are we meeting your other apprentice?" asked Dominic.

"Don't worry, as Barnabus knows about which part of the wall he just needs to know that we must meet, as this is a common meeting place for us, and you will know my apprentice once you and your pet, Leonard, and Barnabus reach the shores of the capital."

"Does your apprentice have a name?"

"Yes, you will know her by her name, Morgana."

With that, Merlin disappeared into what looked like stars, and suddenly Dominic awoke in an uncomfortable position from sleeping sitting up. He looked over to see Leonard asleep and, further to his right, Barnabus sleeping, with his book about to fall from his hands as the fire went out.

4 MEETING BEYOND THE WALL

Dominic got up quickly and ran to Barnabus, waking Leonard in the process. Leonard ran over to Barnabus and barked out loud as Dominic awakened him. Barnabus promptly stood up and grabbed his Jawa Stick next to him.

"What happened?"

"I met Merlin," said Dominic.

Barnabus looked at him curiously.

"What?"

"I met Merlin, and he needs you to meet him quickly,"

"How could you have met Merlin?" asked Barnabus curiously.

"He came to me when I was sleeping," said Dominic.

"He said you must meet him at the high wall near the Spider Witch's castle."

"Ah, I see," said Barnabus.

"Well," said Barnabus, quickly putting the Book of Knowledge into his rucksack and beckoning Dominic to do the same. Dominic gathered items into his bag, and they quietly left the cave.

Dominic, Barnabus, and Leonard hurried along the forest floor. They walked in silence for a while until Dominic cleared his throat. Barnabus walked steadily; he focused on meeting with Merlin but suddenly paused after he looked over at Dominic. He slowed down, as Dominic and Leonard were not used to walking at a Yeti's pace. They went slower, and Dominic looked over at him and was about to say something but stopped. Barnabus saw this and drew out the conversation.

"So, what did you and Merlin discuss?"

Dominic didn't say anything, so Barnabus tried another approach.

"Is there something on your mind?"

They kept walking, then Dominic spoke,

"I don't understand."

"You don't understand, what?" asked Barnabus.

"How, if you and Merlin are great Wizards, that you didn't free all the people and the princess?"

Barnabus didn't say anything; the only answer he could give was the one Dominic had already heard.

"I know what you and Merlin have told me, as I am part of some prophecy, but I know of Merlin at least in my world through the Legend of King Arthur, and you are not only a Wizard but, well," Dominic paused and moved his hand up and down, "You are a Yeti, and I think your site might intimidate some."

Barnabus laughed a little about what Dominic said.

"You know, someone's size doesn't mean everything. I have known many wizards and creatures of Oculus that are much smaller and fiercer than I am."

"But," Barnabus paused, "this isn't bothering you."

"Yes," said Dominic, " I don't understand why you both couldn't save Oculus from the Spider Witch."

"Yes," said Barnabus.

Barnabus stopped.

"I don't like it, but Merlin believes the prophecy."

"But, you and Merlin together are more powerful than I am," said Dominic.

"Dominic, you are more powerful than you think. Don't doubt what you think you know."

They continued walking.

"So, you were an apprentice to Merlin?" asked Dominic.

"Yes, I was one of his first students," said Barnabus.

"What happened to his other students?" asked Dominic.

"Many of his students fought against the Spider Witch, and his students were much like his family. Many died fighting her spider army, but other creatures sided with her. After that day, he wasn't the same and was lost for a while. He came to me in a dream a few months ago about a boy, like you, like the boy from the prophecy. He said he envisioned a boy like you stepping through a wardrobe made of ancient trees from our world."

"I received a wardrobe recently as a gift from my mom," said Dominic.

Barnabus' eyes grew wide, and his smile grew wider.

"Then, that proves it. You are the chosen one."

Dominic looked up, hoping for a sign, but all he saw were the dark clouds from Oculus. Dominic shook his weary thoughts away and asked more questions.

"Why is Merlin meeting us outside the wall? Why not near his home?"

"We always meet there as he feels the Spider Witch would never send her spies or creatures there to 'catch' anyone."

"He mentioned he had something to give you; what is it?" asked Dominic.

"The last time we spoke, he said he was gathering up an army of wizards and rebels to aid in defeating the Spider Witch; when I meet the boy from the prophecy, I suppose that is what the plan is and likely to give more instruction."

Dominic didn't say anything, but Barnabus saw what he was thinking.

"So, who else am I fighting against; I thought it was just spiders and the Spider Witch."

"She has gathered all sorts of creatures besides the Spider Army that came from her land, like goblins, dragons, and even men from the east."

"But why me, or can I help? I am just a boy?"

"You have light and power in you, then you think," said Barnabus.

Dominic nodded as they got closer to the wall. It was dark, and he couldn't see anything. Then, he saw a faint glimmer of what looked like stars forming by the wall. He thought he was hallucinating. Leonard barked, then bounded to the stranger Dominic suddenly saw had appeared in front of them. Leonard licked the man and thought he heard him say, "Good to see you, Leonard." Dominic shook his head and followed after Barnabus, who stood facing the strange man.

The man wore a long blue robe with golden buttons resembling suns. The hood of his cloak covered his face. The man lifted his veil. He had a long, scraggly beard, his hair was long and wildly unkempt, and he looked like he had moss in his hair from how messy his hair looked. What stood out, though, were his eyes, now twinkling and full of hope seeing Barnabus and Dominic.

"Hello there!"

"You must be Merlin," said Dominic, unsure how to respond to this strange Wizard.

"So, master, you said you have something for us?" asked Barnabus.

"Ah, yes, Barnabus, we will get to that, but first, I want to talk to this young lad."

Merlin conjured up a wigwam that blended into the wall to avoid attracting spies. Merlin was the first to step through, then Dominic, Barnabus, and Leonard.

As Dominic came through the opening of the wigwam to get inside, he was surprised to see it was more prominent on the inside than the outside.

It had a fireplace, a carpet on the floor, and a large table with a hosted tea and tea cakes and cookies with a delicious smell and a warm aroma.

"All right, sit down so we can talk."

Everyone sat down as the strange man snapped his fingers, and the tea poured. The tea cakes and cookies floated near Barnabus and Dominic and floated near Leonard as he also sat in the chair next to Dominic.

"Now, I gather you know who I am."

"Yes, based on the last time I saw you and the meeting place, you must be Merlin."

"Spot on, he is, ey Barnabus," said Merlin with a loud chuckle.

"So, why exactly are we here?" asked Dominic.

Dominic stared back at Merlin as if he could see straight through to his very soul.

"I can see you don't like to waste time, and neither do I," said Merlin on a more serious note.

"I can see you don't like my past actions, but I am not going to explain my past, as nothing can be done about the past; only I have to focus on what I can do and what we can all do at present," said Merlin.

"I do, however, like you, young squire. You have noble stock of that; I am certain because you will do your duty."

Barnabus interrupted Merlin and said, "Master, we shave to be on our way soon if we have the opportunity to rid Oculus of the Spider Witch, and you said you had something for me."

"Yes, I do," Merlin said, still stirring his tea.

A sound of feet pattering could be heard outside, and Leonard got in a defensive position and. Dominic felt uneasy, but for some reason, Merlin nor Barnabus got up from their chairs.

"Not to worry, Dominic, anyone looking for us wouldn't be able to get in here," said Barnabus reassured.

"Because of magic," said Dominic.

"Yes, this area is one of the safest, as Merlin's magic is the strongest," said Barnabus.

Merlin droned on about the prophecy and where the sign came from, and all the while, Dominic grew increasingly impatient with Merlin.

"Shouldn't we be on our way now?" asked Dominic.

"Yes, but don't you want to know why I asked you here?" asked Merlin.

Dominic sighed impatiently.

Merlin began to go over the plan of getting into the castle. He told them he was gathering an army over the past few years, as they would need both wit and muscle to defeat the Spider Witch.

"You mean you need an army to go up against her army," said Dominic.

"Who are these men?" asked Barnabus.

"You should know, as she is part of our allies and help get you inside," said Merlin.

It took Barnabus a few seconds to figure out whom Merlin was talking about, and he quickly responded.

"No, no, no, absolutely not."

"You know she was your best pupil and knew the castle's 'ins' and 'outs.'"

"She was also one of my most reckless, rebellious pupils, not to mention obstinate," said Barnabus in a huff folding his arms.

"Excuse me, but whom are you both talking about?" asked Dominic.

"Morgana," they both replied.

"Oh, well, we need to get inside the castle, but I thought she was bad," said Dominic.

"Not bad," said Barnabus, "but one who never followed the rules of magic."

"If she can help us get inside, that isn't a good thing?" asked Dominic.

"It's settled then," said Merlin putting his hand up before Barnabus could object.

"Who else did you get to ally with us?" asked Barnabus.

"A troll or perhaps a dragon," said Barnabus sarcastically.

Merlin cleared his throat and chuckled at Barnabus' comment.

"Only a few dragons."

"What?" exclaimed Dominic.

"Well, I had to add a few new allies," said Merlin with a slight smile.

"Your joking then?" asked Dominic.

"Only a little," said Merlin.

"So, who are our other allies?" asked Barnabus.

"Elves, two dragons, men from the west, and of course, our rebels," said Merlin.

"When do you plan on your attack?" asked Barnabus.

At this time, the tea and cookies were eaten. Merlin got up from his chair and went to the far side of the room. Dominic now noticed on a shelf a pile of books with various titles. He looked around and saw a complete alchemy set percolating on the right side of a table. He saw Merlin hunched over a small chest that lay in the middle. Merlin was busy searching for something.

"What are you searching for?" asked Dominic.

Merlin didn't answer but continued searching through the box.

Then Merlin exclaimed, "Finally, good, I found it."

He pulled out a purple stone, flipped it like a coin, and waved his hand as the rock flew into Barnabus' hands.

"Now, we can go," said Merlin.

"Aren't you forgetting something?" asked Dominic.

Dominic thought Merlin would share his castle battle plans or a better plan of getting inside rather than just telling them to meet Barnabus's apprentice, Morgana, of whom he was unsure about her loyalties.

"Oh, yes," said Merlin.

And with a snap of his fingers, the table, the tea set, the alchemy set, and the books disappeared in a twinkle of starlight.

"No, I mean, of course, but I thought you would share some information about the battle plans or how to get inside the castle, other than just meeting Morgana.

"I entirely agree with Dominic, " said Barnabus.

"Yes, but as my former apprentice, you know what I ask of you and that you should already know; never explain."

"Yes, but a thorough plan leads to more success and fewer errors," said Dominic.

"But, sometimes, you can't waste idle time with planning and explaining you can't try. You have to do it," said Merlin.

Barnabus, Dominic, and even Leonard raised their eyebrows at Merlin and stared at him.

Merlin sighed, turned toward the now empty room, and held out his right hand, and a staff similar to Barnabus' team appeared into his hand. He turned back to them and said,

"All right, let me explain, but we must be quick about this, as Barnabus knows there is a limited time, and time is of the essence."

"What do you mean?" asked Dominic.

Now it was Merlin's turn to raise an eyebrow at Barnabus.

"You haven't told him?" asked Merlin.

"Told me what?" asked Dominic as he turned around to face Barnabus.

Barnabus quickly told Dominic there was only a certain amount of tie as the Spider Witch put a spell that triggered if anyone tried to help the princess.

"If we don't get to the Spider Witch in time, we may lose our memories, and you will be sent back to your world."

"Well then, I think we have wasted enough time drinking tea and having you tell us things," said Dominic.

Merlin cleared his threat, and with a snap of his fingers, the tent folded itself, and Merlin, Barnabus, Dominic, and Leonard were once again outside, but instead of quiet and seeing the wall, they were surrounded by the Spider Witch's army.

Merlin formed a wheel motion with hands pushing his hands forward, and blue light came out of his hands, forcing the giant spider army to be pushed backward.

Barnabus raised his Jawa Staff and vaporized a spider, quickly heading towards Merlin from behind.

"Go!" shouted Merlin at Barnabus, Dominic, and Leonard.

Merlin shot blue light outwards that vaporized a small troll with a club in hand about to knock out Dominic.

"Get out of here, or they will take the boy to her!" shouted Merlin.

Barnabus aimed his Jawa stick outward, looking in all directions for oncoming enemies.

Dominic looked frightened and unsure what he could do while Leonard stood barking and snapping at troll's legs that held clubs as they waved their clubs wildly around.

Leonard barked and looked like he had grown wild as he protected Dominic. While fighting off a giant spider, Merlin saw this and moved one hand toward the spider and another toward the other side where Barnabus, Dominic, and Leonard stood.

Merlin's magic created a bubble just in the nick of time before a giant spider attacked. The bubble surrounded the group as the spiders and trolls surrounded the bubble. That was a close one, pup!" exclaimed Merlin to Leonard.

"Now go, Barnabus. I will push the Spider Witch's army back to give you an opening to leave; I want to meet her, then you must meet Morgana; she will help you get inside.

If I am not there, go with Morgana, as I will lead the troops on as a distraction from the Spider Witch."

25

"Now, go!"

At that moment, Merlin opened the shield and caused the Spider to be pushed backward, giving Barnabus enough time to grab Dominic's hand and Leonard a chance to dash away.

Dominic looked backward for a moment, and to his horror, it looked like the Spider Witch's army had trampled Merlin.

Dominic turned forward as he ran through the forest with all his might.

5 A MERMAID'S TALE

They finally could catch their breath as the spiders were no longer chasing them. As they continued along the path, Barnabus told Dominic more stories about the mermaids. Dominic asked Barnabus about the mermaids.

"These creatures are half-human, half-fish. Many people believe they're not to be trusted, as they have been known to lure sailors or people into the waters, never to return to the surface," said Barnabus.

"They have grown to distrust humans more every day. Now some creatures have taken to siding with the Spider Witch."

"Are they all bad?" Dominic asked.

"No!" exclaimed Barnabus, "Not all of them are bad. Indeed, no!" repeated Barnabus.

"For centuries, as long as we did not bother them, they did not bother us."

Barnabus walked faster and darted about the path. Dominic had to hurry along to keep up with him. Dominic remembered what Barnabus said about the Spider Witch's control of the land. He thought Barnabus was probably trying to confuse anyone who might be watching. Still, Dominic ran as fast as possible to keep up and ask his questions.

"Now," Barnabus said when Dominic caught up, "you need to know more about these creatures to understand Oculus," Barnabus told Dominic of the land of the mermaids.

"The mermaids run the lagoon. The mermaids answer to the mermaid queen to keep order in the lagoon. They do not answer anyone else. The queen gives each mermaid a task. The mermaid queen is chosen through a special ceremony every few years. Each mermaid is assigned a unique role, such as guarding the lagoon, maintaining the coral reefs, or collecting food for the community. These tasks ensure that the mermaid society remains balanced and harmonious."

"How can a mermaid queen be if there was already a king and queen of Oculus?" Dominic interrupted, confused.

"Isn't the mermaid lagoon a part of Oculus?" Barnabus said, "The lagoon is a world within Oculus. It is very similar to how a beehive works. "The mermaids maintain the lagoon under the guidance of the mermaid queen, who ensures order. They do not answer anyone else. The queen assigns each mermaid a specific task."

The path had been winding through tall, dark trees that cast long shadows. As they walked, the temperature rose, and the surroundings transformed into a lush, tropical environment. Dominic and Leonard could feel the warmth in the air, so they took off their winter coats and exchanged them for shorts from their packs. They continued along the path, speaking quietly. Barnabus and Dominic rounded a corner and could now see into the distance. The Spider Witch's castle was within view. In front of the court was the large, dark mermaid lagoon. Barnabus advised Dominic.

"We are close to the lagoon now. If something happens to me on the journey, you must continue alone."

As soon as he said this, he noticed activity near a high wall of the witch's castle.

"I must check this out and make sure we are safe!"

They hurried to the shore of the Black Lagoon.

6 BLACK LAGOON

As they neared the Black Lagoon, Dominic heard a sweet song. Leonard
nudged Dominic with his nose, signaling him to open the harp bag.
Dominic played the harp, and the lagoon's sweet music faded. Dominic
reminded Leonard to stay quiet. They would find themselves in a watery
grave if they made any sound. We have to find a way across the lagoon to
get to the witch's castle, Dominic thought to himself.

Dominic looked over to his right. A boat was tied to the shoreline.
Leonard barked softly and whimpered in protest, but Dominic was
determined to get to the witch's castle to save Princess Rebecca.

They heard the screeching sound of angry mermaids. Barnabus said,
"Once we reach the castle, we will pass a hallway where a wriggle wraith will
guard the Spider Witch's chamber. The wriggle wraiths are creatures that
control people's thoughts. The Spider Witch's chamber they guard is a lost
ideas room. If someone has an idea but then hesitates, their original idea is

lost. The wriggle wraiths will not allow people to have new ideas."

"How do we avoid that?" asked Dominic.

"You have to focus on the task at hand. It would be best if you always stayed in the present. Losing your train of thought and getting distracted is one of the traps the Spider Witch uses to control the land. The only way to defeat the witch is to pass each test by remembering your goal. Remember, your ultimate goal is to help save the lost Princess Rebecca. She is the only one left who can rule Oculus."

"Can you tell me more about the wriggle wraiths?" asked Dominic as they slowly floated across the lagoon.

The small boat rocked back and forth as it navigated the choppy water.

"I will tell you, but remember, this is only for your protection. Before I begin, remember to stay focused and stay in the present," said Barnabus.

"I say this because these creatures will try and keep you from your task. They have a face like a leech, a dog's body, and were bred by the Spider Witch to hunt and feed on her enemies."

Barnabus was about to say more but stopped and said no more as he put his hand closer to his Jawa Staff.

They felt the boat rock and saw a figure peer on the side of the boat. It was hard to see the figure, but the creature screeched as the ship rocked.

"Barnabus, her majesty, the Queen of the Mermaids, wants to see you," hissed the mermaid.

"What a great honor, but we have business with her," said Barnabus, pointing further into the water towards the Spider Witch's castle.

"Yes, you can't keep her waiting, but the Mermaid Queen can't be kept waiting either," said the mermaid.

"We will take you to the Mermaid Queen now."

"How? We can't breathe underwater," said Barnabus.

"We have air bubbles to help you breathe," said the mermaid.

"Come on, let's go."

Dominic looked at Barnabus and boldly said, "We can't trust you because you have drowned people."

"Not to be rude, but we don't know you," said Barnabus.

The mermaid pursed her lips, put her hand in the water, pulled out a water bubble, and pushed the water bubble on Dominic's head.

After placing her hands back on the boat, the mermaid said, "Now, can we get going?"

Barnabus and Dominic didn't move but sat, shocked-faced, unsure what to do next.

The mermaid grabbed another bubble and put it on Barnabus' head. Leonard was the last to get a drop and licked the mermaid while she put it on his head.

She moved and turned toward the water and said, "Come on, let's go."

"Well, are you coming?" the mermaid asked Barnabus and Dominic.

They jumped over the side of the boat into the water.

They followed her as she swam more profoundly into the water, gliding past vibrant kelp forests teeming with a kaleidoscope of fish species until they finally entered the enchanting mermaids' castle. To Dominic's surprise, it was precisely like what Barnabus had described. The palace was white and gold, surrounded by lush kelp vegetation. It was heavily guarded by mermen holding spears. After persuading the guards to let Barnabus, Dominic, and Leonard inside, the mermaid leads the way into the castle.

Once inside, Dominic looked at the Mermaid Queen's castle. It was not like anything he had ever seen. It was ornately decorated with high ceilings, but coral supported the roof instead of high wooden beams. The mermaid led them through a long corridor of rooms, each with a hexagon shape. Dominic, Barnabus, and Leonard didn't walk; they swam through the gallery. Dominic noticed as he looked down; the floor was made of hard rock as he swam.

They swam through the hexagon-shaped corridors until they reached the throne room doors. Two mermen guards on either side blocked the entrances. The guards stood aside to let the Mermaid, Barnabus, Dominic, and Leonard into the throne room. Dominic looked around as they swam into the throne room. He saw a very different person.

The Mermaid Queen was tall with high cheekbones, blond hair wrapped in a tight bun, with an enormous coral crown with sapphires covering the crown. She held a strong image and had a blue and regal tail. She sat on a coral throne with a kelp cushion and stared directly at Dominic. The mermaid that led Barnabus, Dominic, and Leonard swam to the queen and bowed, whispering in the queen's ear. The mermaid moved aside as the queen rose and swam closer to her new visitors.

"So, you are the chosen one," said the Mermaid Queen.

"How do you know?" asked Dominic.

"The water sang to me once you entered my realm," said the Mermaid Queen.

"I have heard stories about you and your people."

"I am sure you have," the Mermaid Queen said with an amused smirk," I am sure it is frightening bedtime stories."

Barnabus was about to speak but was caught off by Dominic's frankness.

"Yes, I have heard your people will cause sailors to drown just by your song."

"I thought as much," said the Mermaid Queen, now circling her guest with an intrigued look.

Barnabus, Dominic, and Leonard were still determining what the Mermaid Queen would do next.

"So, now what?" asked Dominic with a challenging tone.

"Very interesting," The Mermaid Queen said, "Most people are intimidated by me.

"Why should I be?" asked Dominic with a raised eyebrow.

Barnabus quickly changed the subject.

"Why did you call us down here, your majesty?" asked Barnabus with a hint of impatience.

"I called you down here, as I know my people will soon be questioned for our true loyalty, especially since I know this Dominic boy will defeat the Spider Witch," said the Mermaid Queen with a knowing look.

"So, you need us to keep you and your people from punishment?" asked Dominic with a smirk.

The Mermaid Queen moved closer to Dominic, grabbed him by the face, looked him dead in the eyes, and said in a deadly serious voice.

"I do not need anyone to vouch for my people's character. We have never taken anyone's side in this takeover, and I will not have you talk to me in that manner again."

"Your majesty, what exactly do you need us to help you with?" asked Barnabus as he turned his hand towards Dominic placatingly.

"I need you to do what you do best, and that is to create a diversion," said the Mermaid Queen with a sly smile.

"My people need to be protected from blame. I have never sided with either her or your side. What my people need is protection," said the Mermaid Queen.

"What kind of protection?" asked Dominic.

"We need a safe place to live, where we can be free from the judgment of humans. We need a place to be ourselves without pretending to be something we're not.

"My people have old protection missing from my kingdom for many years," said the Mermaid Queen.

"What kind of old protection?" asked Dominic.

"Come," said the Mermaid Queen as she beckoned them.

She swam towards her throne, and Dominic didn't see it before, but she pulled out a large box covered in seashells from the side of their throne.

"This," said the Mermaid Queen, "Is from the beginnings of the time of Oculus, and my people had an ancient protection through a giant squid."

"So, how can I help?" asked Dominic.

She opened the box and pulled out a seashell medallion.

"You will wear this, and when you find our giant squid, bring him to me."

"We need to make a bargain, " said Dominic.

The Mermaid Queen looked puzzled.

"What kind of bargain?" asked the Mermaid Queen.

"One, where we can safely get across your lagoon and find our squid," said Dominic. "This can be arranged," said the Mermaid Queen.

She swam back to her throne, nodded to the mermaid who brought them, and shooed them the way.

"Now remember our bargain, and get out," said the Mermaid Queen. The mermaid that brought them led them out of the Mermaid Queen's throne room, past the guards, and out of the Mermaid Queen's castle back up to the surface towards their boat.

"You know what you must do," said the mermaid.

"Yes, and you know our bargain with the Mermaid Queen," said Dominic.

She pursed her lips, turned, and swam back into the water.

Dominic turned his attention back to the present. The boat rocked gently as Barnabus rowed closer to the shore. Dominic looked towards the lagoon and saw total blackness as far off as possible. He could not see his hand before his face and wondered how Barnabus could row the boat in the right direction. Barnabus looked over to Dominic, who was still playing with the medallion and pensive. Dominic held the medal, played with it, and thought of the bargain with the Mermaid Queen. He didn't know how he could fulfill his part of the bargain, but for now, it helped them get across the black lagoon safely. Barnabus continued rowing across the water as Leonard was asleep at the bottom of the boat.

"What troubles you?"

Dominic said nothing but continued straight ahead, flipping the medallion back and forth on its chain.

"Dominic?" asked Barnabus.

Dominic looked up and said,

"What? Oh, nothing."

Barnabus cleared his throat and continued rowing but didn't say anything. Dominic cleared his throat and sighed,

"I don't know what I am doing here."

"What do you mean?" asked Barnabus.

"I mean, I am just a boy; isn't this for a grown-up?" said Dominic with a hint of uncertainty.

"Well, just Dominic, just because you are a boy doesn't mean anything. What matters is what you do with it. You have a voice and a role to play like anyone. I see someone with more strength and the will to do the right thing than any grown-up," said Barnabus.

"You, a small boy, bravely negotiated a way across a lagoon, and might I add a dangerous lagoon, into the heart of Oculus."

"Never doubt yourself, your grit. That has the strength and wisdom of kings," said Barnabus trying to instill courage in Dominic.

Dominic contemplated momentarily and then asked, "Do you believe I can defeat the Spider Witch?"

"It doesn't matter what I think but what you believe and if you dare to do it," said Barnabus. He continued rowing across the Black Lagoon until they hit a rock.

"Ah," said Barnabus, "we have arrived."

Leonard jumped up as the boat hit the rock. Leonard gave him an almost human nod. Barnabus eyed Leonard and nodded. Barnabus quietly exited the ship, helped Leonard out of the boat with his big yeti hands, and placed him gently on the pebble shore. Dominic was the last to quietly get off the ship as Barnabus led them toward Morgana.

7 MORGANA THE GREAT

Barnabus shoved Dominic out of the water and onto the boat. He
unceremoniously dumped Leonard onto the ship before getting into the
boat and causing it to rock back and forth. Leonard leaped out of the boat
onto the pebble shore and followed along with Dominic. Unlike most dogs,
Leonard made no barking sounds but crept along quietly behind Dominic.
Barnabus needed to be more graceful out of the boat and make the most
noise. His sudden movement made him keenly aware of possible enemy
strongholds, so he pulled his Jawa Staff and surveyed the area.

They moved swiftly to the far side of the castle so as not to attract
attention but close enough to the town to find a way inside. Barnabus
made for the edge where fewer spies or enemies could be lurking. They
made their way toward what looked like the castle sewer system. Around
the sewer lay thick woods. Barnabus crept along as swiftly as a yeti can
advance on a pebble path.

"Barnabus can't you find another path or use your staff to help us to walk silently?" whispered Dominic.

"No one will follow us this way," said Barnabus.

"Why?" asked Dominic.

Barnabus has yet to respond.

They continued walking, then Barnabus turned suddenly toward what looked like a rock or part of a wall formation. Still, Dominic found himself standing in what looked like a bazaar with shops, and when they stepped inside more, he saw in the center of this bazaar a large tent that looked like a circus. "He saw various creatures and animals bustling about. Colorful stalls lined the bazaar, offering exotic trinkets, enchanted artifacts, and a dizzying array of foods that filled the air with tantalizing and peculiar scents.

The atmosphere was buzzing with energy as magical beings chatted animatedly while merchants called out to potential customers, enticing them with their wares. One of the unique types of people looked like extras in a Western movie, complete with hats, spurs, vests, and all manner of Western attire. They were moving around the bazaar, where there were stations with creatures inside. The animals looked like odd creatures found at a circus trapped inside cages. Barnabus stopped suddenly, and Dominic could see an expression of rage on his face. Then, he moved his Jawa Staff toward the cells.

"Bang!"

The cage doors opened, and creatures like centaurs, stags, satyrs, unicorns, and harpies were set free.

"These are free creatures and shouldn't ever be held in prison," said Barnabus.

"Nothing free should ever be controlled or owned."

The creatures slowly emerged from their cages, unsure if they should move.

Dominic cautiously moved one to the satyrs and asked,

"Who are you, and who put you in this prison?"

"I am Pip, and this is Flute," said the Satyr.

"The ring leader put us in the cages as a spectacle close to the circus entrance."

"Who is the ring leader?" asked Dominic.

"She created this part of Oculus. It's a sort of 'haven' for criminals or rebels. It was created when the Spider Witch came to power."

"Then, how did you know this place?" asked Barnabus.

"My brother and I were captured by the ring leader and made to work for her as an amusement for her circus."

While Dominic was asking questions, Barnabus was growing angrier and angrier. Leonard saw this and put his paw on Barnabus' leg, and Dominic could see that Leonard shook his dog's head as Barnabus held the Jawa Staff, and the staff started to glow.

Barnabus felt Leonard's paw and checked himself.

"Where does the ring leader live?" asked Barnabus.

Flute pointed towards the large tent that Dominic saw when they entered the bazaar. He saw the giant sign on the top of the circus tent, with oversized lettering and an audacious gold coloring, "The Big Top."

"She is about to start one of her shows, and it usually has some traditional oddities like the Bearded Lady, the Strong Man, a few clowns, elephants, and even fighting bears," said Pip.

"I still don't understand what kind of place this is," said Dominic.

"It is a place that some of the people that are either rebel needing a place to hide or those that are of the low life of Oculus that managed to evade the Spider Witch's powers," said Barnabus.

Dominic was surprised by Barnabus' response.

"How do you know about this place?" asked Dominic.

"I know this place as the person who runs this place was someone I once knew," said Barnabus.

As Barnabus had said, he had been busy looking at the tent with the "Big Top" sign.

"You keep staring at the sign; why don't we go inside?" asked Dominic.

Barnabus thought about this and cleared his throat,

"Yes," said Barnabus, "it's time I paid the Ring Leader a visit."

They were still talking to Pip and Flute; when some knights in black armor approached them.

"What are you doing out of your cage?"

Pip and Flute shook with fear and were dumbfounded.

"We, uh.."

"What they mean to say is the Ring Leader spoke to us and said they would go on next, but before that, she let them out to show us around," said Dominic.

"Really?" asked one of the knights.

"Yes, we were heading into The Big Top right now, and the satyrs were going to escort us there," said Dominic.

"How about we escort you all to the Big Top," said one of the knights.

"That's okay. We can manage on our own," said Barnabus.

"No, we insist," said the knight, "hey, where did you get that?"

"Get what?" asked Barnabus.

"That," said the knight pointing to Barnabus' Jawa Staff.

The knight reached out to grab the Jawa Staff, stopped suddenly, and looked back at the other knights, dazed.

"Well, come on, let's go; they have everything handled here," said the knight.

They turned and went into a shop that sold odd spices. Once the knights were out of earshot, Dominic turned towards Barnabus.
"What was that about?" asked Dominic.

"I thought we were goners for sure. Why did they turn suddenly and leave?"

"One of the many benefits of being a wizard," said Barnabus with a cheeky grin.

"Shall we go?"

"Go? Go where?" asked Dominic.

Barnabus pointed with his Jawa Staff.

"To the Big Top, of course."

Barnabus asked Pip and Flute to lead the way so the group would look less suspicious with Pip and Flute out of their cages.

"Well, this is where we part," said Barnabus.

"We would, but where would we go?" asked Flute.

"We are prisoners with the Spider Witch or here with the Ring Leader," said Pip.

"You know that out of here, others are fighting against the Spider Witch; in fact, Merlin is putting together an army to fight against her," said Dominic.

Barnabus turned and gave Dominic a look as if to say quietly.

"Yes, and if all goes well, you and more people like you will be free soon," said Dominic, ignoring Barnabus' look.

Dominic turned to Barnabus defiantly.

"Well, they asked."

"How do we find them?" asked Pip.

"Go out of this tent carefully, and as soon as you are out of here, meet Merlin at the far side of the castle wall," said Barnabus.

"Tell him a friend who still believes in him sent you."

"Since you are a wizard, don't you have some way for Pip and Flute not to be seen?" asked Dominic.

Barnabus gently turned his Jawa Staff towards Flute and Pip. Dominic's eyebrows rose in surprise as Pip and Flute seemed to disappear.

"Where did they go?" asked Dominic.

"They're there," said Barnabus pointing toward the space that Flute and Pip occupied.

"Flute, Pip, are you there?" asked Dominic.

"Yes, we are here," said Flute and Pip in unison.

"You better hurry," said Barnabus, "As that spell tends to wear off quickly."

"Right, we can't thank you enough," said Flute and Pip.

Dominic heard footsteps moving away and felt relief for his new friends.

Barnabus moved into the Big Top, with Dominic and Leonard following quickly.

Once inside, the room was different from what Dominic would have expected. It was very well-lit with large crystal chandeliers, and instead of dirt floors, the floors were made of black and white marble. Instead of bleacher seats, they had proper theatre seats with red cushions, like those you would find at an opera.

The unique aspect that Dominic observed was that, unlike a typical circus where everyone picked a seat, there were ushers with flashlights clipping customer tickets to particular rows of seats like in a theatre. Each usher wore a uniform adorned with intricate patterns and vibrant colors, giving them an air of elegance and professionalism.

So, this made a slight difficulty in Dominic's mind, as they hadn't purchased any tickets until Dominic remembered Barnabus' Jawa Staff.

Barnabus shouldn't we sit up at the front, so we can see if we can find the Ring leader, and she can help us find Morgana?" asked Dominic.

"And, anyway, where are we going to get tickets?"

"Not to worry, we will have one of the ushers help us," said Barnabus.

An usher with blond hair dressed like a bellhop approached them. He had a red suit with gold buttons and stripes down his red suit. His was a red box-shaped cap with a black leather strap so tight under his chin that it made the usher's face scowl.

"Tickets, please," said the usher with a sigh.

"Uh, tickets, right? Barnabus, you have our tickets, right?" asked Dominic nervously.

"Yes, I have them right here," said Barnabus pulling out three tickets with their seat number and name.

The usher took their tickets and punched a hole, In them, then pointed his flashlight toward three front-row seats close to what Dominic could now see as an orchestra pit.

The theatre was packed. Though not of the variety of creatures from outside of the Big Top, but of humans or what look like humans; however, in the orchestra pit, there were elves tuning mandolin guitars and violins.

"There were talking pigs on drums, their snouts bobbing in rhythm as they tested the beat. Fairies flitted around trumpets, their tiny fingers delicately tuning the instruments, while bears stood on their hind legs, expertly adjusting the saxophones with their enormous paws.

Barnabus, Dominic, and even Leonard took their seats in the front row, waiting for the show to start.

The room became dark, and an eerie mist filled the air. Suddenly, a booming, captivating voice echoed throughout the stage area,

"Ladies and gentlemen, boys and girls, prepare to be mystified, mesmerized, and amazed by the wonders you are about to witness!"

The light flickered all over the stage and landed on the center, where two prominent figures appeared. The lights on the stage grew brighter for a better view of the figures. The location was transformed into a ring like a boxing ring.

Dominic saw who the figures were. They were two giant grizzly bears wearing Jiujitsu Gis.

"And now, our undefeated champion weighing three hundred pounds and wearing a red Gi, Smokey Bones."

And Dominic saw the bear lift his arms to show off to the crowd's cheering.

"And our newest challenger, weighing in at three hundred and fifty pounds, wearing a blue Gi, Captain Smalls."

Dominic saw this bear, who had a fiercer expression and a look of determination, suddenly growl, and the crowd started booing.

"Will Smokey Bones have another win, or will we have a new winner today?" asked a voice coming from a speaker from the theatre.

"Okay, let's find out; ready, set, fight!"

Suddenly, a referee appeared from the bottom of the stage. The referee was a petit figure wearing a mask and a ref outfit in black and purple with long black hair and bits of purple braided and tied in a tight bun.

The fighting between the two bears began. Smokey Bones sized up his new opponent. Dominic suddenly heard the voice again, sharing the play-by-play in the theatre.

"It looks like Smokey Bones is sizing up his opponent. He and Captain Smalls seem to be circling one another to see who will make the first move."

Then out of nowhere, Captain Smalls went in with his first move.

"Oh, Captain Smalls is going in with his first move. They are starting with a Judo Grip to get away with a clean sweep. But Smokey Bones is an old pro at this; he quickly gets out of the grip and trips Captain Smalls pinning him on the mat. Will Captain Smalls get free? Let's find out?"

Dominic fidgeted with his ticket, his excitement growing, and he couldn't help but yell out, "Come on, Captain Smalls!"

The ref looked in Dominic's direction, and Dominic could see a slight frown but saw the ref quickly focused back on the two bears.

Dominic saw this led Captain Smalls was able to get somehow free.

"Captain Smalls got free and is now stalking Smokey Bones, making good leg work with his sweep, and knocked Smokey Bones down."

"As the fight continued, Dominic noticed the referee discreetly extending her finger toward the bears. Suddenly, Smokey Bones' eyes changed to purple, and he pinned Captain Smalls with a quick arm bar.

The crowd cheered as the announcer or what looked like the referee. "We have a winner!"

"Our undefeated champion, Smokey Bones!"

Dominic heard the click of gold coins thrown by people in the audience onto the ring. Dominic was about to say something they saw the referee snap her fingers, and the call changed, and the ring was lowered. The crew changed to a marble stage, which was dark until the orchestra started again.

The light fell around the stage as clowns and elephants were somehow walking into the Big Top led by the same masked person, but this time she was wearing what could be described as ringmaster attire. Her attire was a black gentlemen's top coat in black and purple, and black waistcoat, black trousers, and purple high boots like a ringmaster would wear. She had a large black top hat with a royal purple rim.

Dominic found unique about this ringmaster: instead of just bounding through like everyone else, she flew through the air on a trapeze swing. She landed like a sharp point right in the middle of the stage, with a pose like a court jester performing their final act. Her hands were raised above her head, and one foot was pointed in front of her other foot. Her facial expression was that of a cat getting the cream as the crowd cheered.

The orchestra sounded like a loud old jazz band, and as the ringmaster lowered her arms, the orchestra grew softer as she introduced more of the circus acts.

Each act was what Dominic or anyone from our world would expect from a circus. There was the bearded lady, elephants, clowns spraying water in one another's faces, and the strong man and the ringmaster swinging on the trapeze.

The difference was that the goblins acted like clowns spraying water in each other's faces. Minotaur was jumping through fiery hoops or harpies flying through the theatre.

Each time a new act was introduced, Dominic would look over to Barnabus and look up at the ringmaster. It looked as though Barnabus recognized the ringmaster, and Dominic noticed the ringmaster would scowl at Barnabus after an act was introduced. Then the ringmaster would quickly put on her charisma for the audience. Just as the show began, it was soon over with a snap of the Ring Master's fingers. A purple cannon appeared, and the two bears placed her inside the gun. One of the bears, still wearing his red Gi, took a torch and lit the cannon's wick on fire; that shot the Ring Master out of the gun, and a cloud of purple smoke hovered over the stage. As soon as the smoke cleared, everything and everyone disappeared. Barnabus, Dominic, and Leonard were once again sitting in a quiet theatre with ushers busy clearing everyone out and cleaning up.

"Well, I think it's time to meet this Ring Master," said Barnabus.

The stage was now empty, and the theatre lights were dim. The ushers came by, busy cleaning up the aisles. Soon, the usher with the tight cap that had helped them to their seats came up, telling them to leave.

Barnabus ignored him.

"Where can we find the Ring Master?" asked Barnabus.

"If you go across this stage, her dressing room is at the very end, but you can't go back there," said the usher in a bored tone.

"But, didn't you know that she invited us there," said Dominic.

The usher rolled his eyes and sighed.

"That is what everyone says. Someone always wants to meet her. Well, you can't. " Go as the show is over, and it is time for me to get off my shift," said the usher.

The usher was sweaty with poor posture and kept shooing Dominic, Barnabus, and Leonard out of the theatre, but they wouldn't budge.

Leonard barked and stood in between Barnabus and the usher.

"Great," said the usher, "Now, I have to clean as you brought your dog in here."

"Well, he doesn't seem to like you, so if you let us through, we can be out of your way soon," said Dominic, standing with his arms crossed.

Barnabus quickly moved closer to the user to prevent him from saying anything else to Dominic.

"You seem like a hard-working fellow," said Barnabus, "Tell me, what is your name?"

"Yes, you are right; I am one of the hardest-working people here," said the usher.

"I have to work and take everyone's tickets, take them to their seats; it is so exhausting, and no one appreciates all that I do."

Barnabus cleared his throat, slightly annoyed by the whining from the usher, but kept on with the conversation to distract him. While Barnabus let the usher drone on and on as a pity party, Barnabus moved them closer to the stage.

"So tell me, fellow, what is your name?" asked Barnabus.

"My name is Rudy."

"I understand where you are coming from about not feeling appreciated; that is why we are seeing our friend, the Ring Master," said Barnabus.

"Tell me, my friend, Rudy, would you prefer to do something else?" asked Barnabus.

Rudy paused and turned to Barnabus.

"What?" asked Rudy.

"No, I am better than any job I can get here, don't you understand? I am not appreciated enough for all I have to do here."

Dominic tapped his foot as he grew impatient, listening to Rudy complain.

"So, what would you like to do?" asked Barnabus, gently nudging Rudy to continue walking.

"Well, I want to be one of the show's performers, " Rudy said as his eyes lit up.

"Ah, now we are getting somewhere," said Barnabus as they walked onto the stage, and the sound of shoes and yeti feet could be heard echoing through the theatre.

"What are your talents?" asked Barnabus.

"Well, I don't want to brag," said Rudy, as he tried to show modesty but failed.

"Yes," said Barnabus.

"But I have so many."

"Like," Barnabus said, waving his hand to get Rudy to continue.

Barnabus paused and aimed his staff at the empty orchestra pit, and the music started playing. Barnabus aimed his Jawa Staff at the spotlight on the stage, and the spotlight aimed straight at Rudy.

"Show us your talents," said Barnabus.

"I will in time, but first, you need to do something for me," said Rudy.

"What can we do for you?" asked Barnabus.

"Put a good word in for me so I can join her performers."

Barnabus looked thoughtfully and nodded.

"But to put a good word in for you, we first have to meet her, so you have to take us to her," said Dominic.

Rudy narrowed his eyes directly at Dominic.

"Fine!" exclaimed Rudy.

Rudy walked towards the Ring Master's door with Barnabus, Dominic, and Leonard trailing behind.

Rudy leads them through a hallway to the Ring Master's dressing room.

It wasn't a typical hallway. The walls had a variety of loud colors and a new portrait of the Ring Master on both sides of the walls going towards the end of the hallway up to the Ring Master's door. As Rudy, Barnabus, Dominic, and Leonard walked. Dominic noticed the floor was black and white and turned sideways.

"Is it me, or does this room seem to be getting longer, or are we getting smaller?" asked Dominic.

"No, didn't you know everything has to get smaller before it can get larger," Rudy continued leading them to the Ring Master.

They stood right outside of the Ring Master's door.

It wasn't like an average stage door; it, like so many things the Ring Master owned or wore, was painted royal purple.

The door handle had a golden handle shaped like a hand, and the peephole looked like a giant eyeball watching in every direction.

What came next made even the calm Barnabus jump. The eye of the peephole started talking.

"Oh, hello there."

Barnabus, Dominic, and Leonard jumped back. Rudy stood, surprised by their reaction.

"Oh, I get that a lot," said the eye.

Dominic saw that the eye had a knocker that moved like a mouth as the eye moved back and forth.

"So, why are you all here?" asked the eye.

"We want to see the Ring Master," said Dominic.

"Ha!"

The eye blinked, and its door mouth laughed.

"Everyone wants to see her. You wouldn't believe the kind of excuses I get, so someone could see the Ring Master and how hard my job is to keep people out."

The eye looked down, almost sad, thinking about his job.

"What exactly do you do?" asked Dominic.

"I give people a riddle, and if they guess wrong, which happens often, then my door opens, and if they walk through, they all through an oubliette where they are never seen or heard from again."

"What is an oubliette?" implored Dominic.

"It, like its name, means to forget, and the person falls through a dungeon or the deepest part of it."

"Um, Barnabus, are you sure about this?" asked Dominic.

"I don't like being forgotten," said Dominic.

Barnabus moved forward and gave Dominic a reassuring pat on the shoulder.

"We want to make an effort with your riddle," said Barnabus.

Barnabus heard Rudy clear his throat.

"And that you will include Rudy if we are successful."

"I won't be included if you are not, I hope?" asked Rudy.

"No, of course not," said Barnabus.

"Well, of course, he wouldn't, as he is one," the eye paused.

Barnabus looked over at Rudy as he shook his head.

"Shall we begin?" asked the eye.

Barnabus nodded.

"What can you break without using your hands?"

Barnabus paused and stood still with his Jawa Staff out like that of a cane for an older man.

"Um, Barnabus, aren't you? Going to answer?" asked Dominic.

Barnabus didn't answer, and Dominic started to panic. He looked over at Rudy and noticed Rudy was smirking.

"A heart, cheese, time," said Dominic.

"Are those your answers?" asked the eye.

"Um, Barnabus, what is it?" asked Dominic.

"Time is almost out," said the eye.

47

Then out of nowhere, Barnabus answered.

"A promise," said Barnabus.

Rudy looked to see between the eye and Barnabus, surprised.

"That's correct," said the eye, "You may pass through."

The first to go through was Barnabus through a haze of purple mist, followed by Dominic and Leonard.

Rudy was last to go through, but the mist blocked him as soon as he stepped through.

"Hey, come on!" exclaimed Rudy.

"You know the rules," said the eye as the door closed.

"That isn't fair," said Rudy, "You made a deal."

"Yes, they got to go inside as the Ring Master planned."

"Yes, and I did as she asked me to do, but you said I could go through," said Rudy, "As I wanted to be part of her performance."

Rudy gritted his teeth and stomped away.

The eye on the door turned purple, and the knocker's mouth smiled slyly.

Barnabus stepped through the purple mist with his Jawa Staff as a beacon. Dominic and Leonard followed closely behind. Once inside, the room was different from what I expected. The room was more significant than Dominic had expected it to be.

The was brightly lit with sizeable ornate crystal chandeliers, lush carpets, and plush furniture, all decorated in purple.

A reception desk was at the front of this room, which seemed to go on forever. There was a petite woman with black hair and a bit of a purple streak tied in a tight bun. She wore purple-rimmed glasses. She wore a black and purple pinstripe suit and typed at her desk. The only sound heard was the typewriter's click, click. The woman only looked up at Barnabus with a deep scowl.

"Yes, may I help you?" said the secretary.

"Hello, ahem, what is your name?" asked Barnabus.

The secretary looked straight at Barnabus, and Dominic noticed she had bits of purple flecks in her eyes.

Dominic traveled at lightning speed through the Spider Witch's castle sewer tunnels. The ride would have been more shocking had he, not Ring

Master and Morgana, been one in the same person. Dominic sat on what can be described as a giant roller-skate track. He and Leonard were tied with white shoelaces to prevent falling out of a carnival ride-style seat. The roller-skate vehicle had whole peep windows from where laces would typically tie, and Dominic had to keep looking straight ahead to prevent himself from getting motion sickness, by how fast Morgana was powering the roller-skate. Dominic looked straight at Barnabus, who stood overhead, watching over Morgana as she powered the roller skate.

Morgana and Barnabus stood before a large furnace, similar to an old steam-engine locomotive. Still, it was powered by Morgana's magic instead of coal powering the roller skate.

Morgana and Barnabus stood silently, a change from their constant bickering hours before.

"No, absolutely not," said Barnabus, still standing with his Jawa Staff in hand. Barnabus loomed over Morgana as she was still tied to the sofa chair.

"What do you mean no?" asked Morgana.

"I heard Merlin quite well enough," said Morgana, "He wanted me to accompany you, likely to protect you more than the boy as you are getting older, old man."

Morgana was testing Barnabus' patience, and soon, the Jawa Staff started to grow again, and the sofa arms grew tighter around Morgana.

"We don't have time for your bad jokes, apprentice," said Barnabus, now goading Morgana.

"We must find a way inside the Spider Witch's castle."

"The sofa arms made it difficult for Morgana to speak. Dominic realized this and began to intervene.

"Hey, Barnabus, I don't think choking Morgana will help the quest, and I don't think this is something Merlin wanted you to do."

Dominic gingerly touched Barnabus' arm. Barnabus snapped out of his angry mood, checked himself, and the components of the sofa opened up, allowing Morgana to stand up as she breathed deeply. Morgana breathed in and out slowly as she steadied herself.

"Well, old man, you haven't changed much."

"The boy is correct, and Merlin wouldn't want you to do that."

"Now, on to business."

She moved to the far side of a well-lit bookshelf pulled onto a wall sconce, and the wall to the library moved to a small opening. Morgana stepped through and turned towards Dominic, Barnabus, and Leonard.

"Well, come on then, let's not wait for the grass to grow."

Dominic followed Morgana through the secret passage. Once he stepped through, he saw the room wasn't a room but a sewer with what looked like a track found at a fairground, like a roller coaster track.

Dominic looked around, and on the walls, he saw a brightly lit torch in a perfect row throughout the long sewer.

He heard Leonard come through with his soft paws, and Barnabus came with a loud thump.

Dominic continued looking around at the scene before him and noticed at the far end of the tracks a larger-than-life roller-skate and a ladder than life roller skate and a ladder leading up to the front of the door of the roller-skate.

He was still surprised by the roller skate size that he didn't notice the conversation or argument between Barnabus and Morgana, nor Leonard's growling and lurking at Morgana.

"What on earth is that?" asked Barnabus.

"It is a roller skate, of course," said Morgana.

"Yes, I know that, but why is it here, and why aren't we traveling on foot?" asked Barnabus.

"Why would we travel by foot," asked Morgana.

"To not alert her army of spiders or other allies, of course," said Barnabus.

"That wouldn't make sense," said Morgana, "especially when Merlin approved how we travel."

Morgana smirked at this, and Barnabus sighed and shook his head.

"When will you share the rest of Merlin's plan with us?" asked Barnabus.

"When I feel like it, old man," said Morgana.

Dominic saw that Barnabus was upset and set out to calm him down and get on with the quest.

"So, Morgana, how do we get inside this roller skate?" asked Dominic.

This distracted both Morgana and Barnabus.

"Just climb up the ladder, and there is a side door up the top."

Dominic was the first to climb the ladder, and Morgana followed. Barnabus picked up Leonard with his giant yeti hands, carefully placed Leonard in the crook of his arm, and held his Jawa Staff as he pulled onto the ladder.

Dominic continued walking up the ladder and started getting red hands and bits of calluses as he walked up the rope ladder. His hands and body began to sweat as he grabbed hold of the rope and slowly reached the top bit red-faced and out of breath.

"You must not be used to physical exercise," said Morgana.

Dominic paused and entered the roller skate, opening what looked like a door.

He waited until Morgana and Barnabus got inside, and as soon as Barnabus put Leonard down, he spoke to Morgana.

"Now, look here, you have some issues to resolve with Barnabus, but you have taken a verbal swipe at him and now myself," said Dominic.

"But the only way we can win and free this land, its people, and the princess is by working together."

"So, no more little jibes at Barnabus or me."

Morgana, at first, was stunned and turned and raised an eyebrow at Barnabus, thinking Barnabus had coached him to say that, but soon realized Dominic had a mind of his own.

Morgana was silent but admired Dominic's cheek.

"So, Barnabus, you have a new apprentice," said Morgana.

She paused and, still holding her wizard staff, directed them to sit as she used her magical team to start up the roller skate engine if there was one.

The engine would have been part of the toe of the skate; however, never used differently. It had a furnace like that of a steam engine locomotive, and instead of coal power and heat, it operated only by Morgana's magic.

Morgana shot with her wizard staff at the furnace, and the giant roller skate jerked forward and began to move. It slowly moved, but as Morgana added more magic from her team, it began to pick up speed and travel faster. He first noticed that it wasn't traditional roller skate. It had crystal chandeliers and grand carnival seating.

At first, it was a silent journey where no one said anything. Barnabus,

Dominic, and Leonard sat in what looked like seats from a carnival or rollercoaster.

Morgana stood next to the furnace. Her staff stood in a hole and acted like the wheel on a ship to help her steer. Barnabus sat and looked out of the shoelace window, trying to see the direction of the roller skate.

Leonard paced in the seat, finally relaxed, and slowly drifted asleep.

Dominic sat and observed both Barnabus and Morgana.

Morgana continued steering the roller skate like a captain on a ship, and once they got to a consistent speed, she took her hand away from her staff. The staff had a purple glow surrounding her team as the roller skate continued to move. Morgana turned around and had her back now against what would be the side of the roller skate.

Dominic observed her eyes darting between Barnabus and himself.

Dominic broke the silence.

"So, you were Barnabus' apprentice?" asked Dominic.

"Yes, and thankful to have moved on from that," said Morgana, looking at Barnabus' reaction.

Dominic paused but continued staring at Morgana as if seeing through her.

"Why do you ask?" asked Morgana.

"Well, this seems like a long journey, and I don't know much about you or even Barnabus," said Dominic.

"So, to pass the time?" asked Morgana.

"Very well," said Morgana.

Barnabus turned away from the window and faced Morgana as she retold her apprenticeship.

"Like all stories, my story ended not so happily," said Morgana.

She paused and cleared her throat.

"I came from a small town in the western part of Oculus. I had never heard or seen magic nor been to the capital.

One day, Barnabus came to my town. He looked strange in his wizard robes and yeti fur. He came to my village searching for a new wizard apprentice. Barnabus was getting frustrated with finding apprentice recruits and wasn't used to the weather out west. One scorching day, as I was drawing water from the town; well, Barnabus was parched of thirst, and I gave him water.

Out of nowhere, a child ran into the street simultaneously; a runaway coach came through the main road. The child and stagecoach were about to collide as the coach got closer. I raised my hands, and all the people and objects stopped.

My eyes were closed, and I felt a large hand pat my shoulder.

"How did you know to do the freeze spell?" asked Barnabus.

"I, I, I don't know," said Morgana.

"I didn't want the little girl to get hurt."

"Hmmm, interesting," said Barnabus.

"I think I have found my new apprentice."

Morgana went on to tell Dominic that since she had no living family, she was happy to find a friend who could share her magical abilities.

"Why did you have a falling out with Barnabus?" asked Dominic.

"I am getting to that," said Morgana.

She looked to Barnabus, who was strumming his hands over his Jawa Staff.

"Well, I need to get to that point," said Morgana.

Barnabus took me in and quickly put me to work as his apprentice," said Morgana.

"Did you get to practice spells or make potions?" asked Dominic.

"Not really," said Morgana, "I spent most of my time cleaning up his study, washing potion bottles, or being told how I am not controlling my wizard staff correctly."

"But that still doesn't explain why you are upset with Barnabus," said Dominic, "as an apprentice, you have to take orders from your master."

Barnabus smiled at Dominic, and his eyes twinkled toward Morgana.

"Of course, but the biggest issue came later when the Spider Witch came," said Morgana.

"What do you mean?" asked Dominic.

"Do you remember how Barnabus was banished?" asked Morgana.

"Barnabus didn't tell you what because of his apprentice."

"Yes," said Barnabus, "You could fill me in on that one."

"Ahem," said Morgana, "so before the Spider Witch came, all of the king's advisors tried to figure out how to beat her, either through magical means or military strength."

"And which did you choose?" asked Dominic.

"Well, I didn't choose," said Morgana, "it was the advisors, one of which was Barnabus, and it was through both magical and military might."

"The strategy that Barnabus chose was he and I would face the Spider Witch and her at the castle, though I wanted the family to be rescued or safely in exile, and we use our other magical allies to push the Spider Witch back."

Morgana sighed and faced the furnace.

"Of course, you know whose plan was chosen," said Morgana, "after that, I was left on my own."

"And this is where I had to fend for myself," said Morgana, "and make backroom deals with people like the Spider Witch."

Barnabus stood up, now in a defensive pose. This shook the roller skate and caused the roller skate to rock from side to side.

Leonard woke with a jolt, ended up on the floor of the roller skate, and whimpered. Dominic immediately shot up and ran to help Leonard.

"Now, see what you have done," said Morgana.

"You always leave the weaker to suffer."

"Suffer!" exclaimed Barnabus, now face to face with Morgana.

"Ta!"

"You wouldn't even know the word."

"Really?" exclaimed Morgana.

"Yes, really," said Barnabus, "especially if you are a double agent for the Spider Witch."

"I bet you are taking her to us right now."

"You believe that, especially when you abandoned me!" exclaimed Morgana, her eyes growing more purple the angrier she got.

"Why else would you hold creatures of Oculus captive or use them for money?"

"Oh, that," said Morgana.

"Oh, that is right," said Barnabus.

"They are there because she was planning on feeding mystical creatures to here on feeding mystical creatures to her spider army and any of her other allies; the only bargain I could make with her was imprisonment."

54

"Why not let them join Merlin's army?" asked Barnabus.

"Because, when I allied, as you put it, there wasn't an army until recently," said Morgana.

Morgana moved towards Leonard to check on the pup and heal him. She helped Dominic up and gently handed Leonard to him.

Dominic gently put Leonard on his seat.

"Thank you," said Dominic.

Morgana was surprised by Dominic's sincerity.

"Well, at least someone can show respect," said Morgana.

Barnabus just grunted.

"So, you thought you would be helpful and house all the mythical creatures of Oculus, and you got money for being a philanthropist?" asked Barnabus.

"How else could I house and feed them all?" asked Morgana.

"By not using them as an opportunity to gain money," said Barnabus.

"Well, you weren't here. How else should I care for everyone and myself?" asked Morgana.

"You are working for her," said Barnabus, as his big frame overshadowed her petite frame.

"That," said Morgana, "is a cover to ensure those creatures are safe."

"How can we be sure you are telling the truth?" asked Barnabus.

She now got toe to toe with Barnabus.

"You just going to have to trust me," said Morgana.

She turned and steered the roller skate once more.

That seemed hours ago as Dominic was brought back to the present moment. Neither Morgana nor Barnabus were saying anything and wouldn't look at one another. Dominic broke the silence by asking questions.

"So, once we get to wherever we are going, how are we going to find her, and how are we going to defeat her?" asked Dominic.

"And, why is it taking so long to get there?" asked Dominic, "I thought we were by the Spider Witch's Castle."

"One question at a time," said Morgana," First, Merlin didn't share any other information with me, and second, it is because we passed through my realm, much like you went through a portal from your world."

"And, as I have had my share of dealings with the Spider Witch, there are several ways to get inside, but since you don't want to be seen, the best way to travel is through the kitchen."

"I see, but isn't the kitchen going to be full of her creatures and stuff?" asked Dominic.

"Yes, but we will only have to worry about a big troll that acts as her chef," said Morgana.

"A troll!" exclaimed Dominic.

"Yes, but I am sure the great Barnabus can help us with that," said Morgana with a smirk.

"I think Morgana can handle him well enough, as it seems you had some near misses with the troll," said Barnabus sarcastically.

Morgana pursed her lips and didn't respond.

"Well, aren't you going to share with us how to move past this troll," said Barnabus.

"When you were comfortable in exile, I helped rescue creatures from being eaten," said Morgana.

Dominic quickly changed the subject.

"Did Merlin mention anything else?" asked Dominic.

"He wants us to signal his men once we are inside," said Morgana.

"How?" asked Dominic.

"With a fire from the kitchen, of course," said Morgana, rolling her eyes.

"You mean you set the kitchen on fire?" asked Dominic, confused.

"She means to use our staffs and create a wizard fire, similar to what you see here," said Barnabus pointing to the furnace that powered the roller skate.

Morgana looked up and put her head out of the shoelace window.

"We are almost there."

"One thing I still don't understand is why it is taking so long to get there, as it is technically in the Spider Witch's castle," said Dominic.

"This roller skate, or rather us traveling from my world to the Spider Witch's actual part of her castle, helps to create a vortex or portal, much like the portal I assume you traveled through."

"I see," said Dominic.

"But how are we going to sneak past the troll?" asked Dominic.

"Easy, very carefully," said Morgana.

Barnabus and Dominic rolled their eyes; Even Leonard shook his head and put his paw over his eyes.

"What is the real way to get past the troll?" asked Dominic.

"We have to push the grate that connects to the sewer carefully. It is a kitchen, so you can imagine how busy it will be, and before opening the grate, we have to watch out for her spies that pace the sewer," said Morgana.

"So, once we get inside, how do we get past the troll and out where any other trolls or spiders won't see us?" asked Dominic.

"The troll that guards the kitchen is almost the size of a giant. He hangs out by a large black cauldron where he makes his favorite dishes, but it smells like rotting garbage," said Morgana, " We should be fine if we can quietly go past when his back is turned."

They traveled along the tracks in the roller skating at a much faster pace. What struck Dominic was that even though they were going past the Spider Witch's guards, etc., they weren't being chased or noticed.

Morgana had strategically parked her roller skate just under the sewer that connects to a gate that leads to the kitchen.

"How come trolls and spiders aren't bombarding us?" asked Dominic.

At this point, steam or what looked like steam but magic from Morgana's wizard staff blew across the floor of the roller-skate out towards the trolls, and the trolls stopped briefly near the roller-skate.

Morgana looked out of the roller-skate window and used her staff towards the troll, and the troll shook its head and went back to marching.

"Getting a little rusty, aren't we," said Barnabus.

"Not at all, old man," said Morgana.

Dominic exhaled sharply.

"Can anyone tell me what just happened and why the trolls and spiders haven't come yet to imprison or eat us?" asked Dominic.

Morgana moved to the seat where Dominic stood, shot her wizard staff straight up, and uncovered or gently unrolled the roof. It parted the large chandelier and revealed a large grate, letting waste and water into the roller skate.

"That can't be good," said Dominic as he picked up Leonard.

"The reason her creatures can't see us; is there is a cloaking spell, and the reason the trolls stopped is that some of my magic drifted out, and the trolls have a great sense of smell towards magic or magical objects," said Morgana, "That is why I placed a confused spell on him so he would forget what he was doing."

"They are rather thick, so they are easy to mess with," said Morgana, smirking.

The grate sliced open quietly with the use of Morgana's Wizard staff.

She slid the lid up and quietly emerged with her head peaking for upcoming enemies. She fully appeared and beckoned for Dominic, still holding Leonard, to follow.

Dominic whispered," I am too short to get into the kitchen."

Morgana leaked down through the gaping hole where Dominic stood.

"Barnabus let the kid up, as he isn't ready yet," said Morgana.

Barnabus picked Dominic up with one yeti hand and threw Dominic in the air, with Dominic gripping Leonard hard. Morgana quickly caught Dominic with one and pulled him inside through the kitchen grate.

Once Barnabus emerged with a slight thud echoing through the kitchen, Dominic hid and took in his surroundings.

He saw piles and piles of dirty dishes teetering from side to side. He saw the floor had bits of old food and stickiness from an old mop layer with cobwebs in the corner. The room didn't have a pleasant smell as a typical kitchen would. It had a musty odor like that of old gym socks.

Dominic saw it was a messy kitchen; ironically, no one seemed to notice them. Dominic whispered to Morgana, did you put an invisibility spell on us?"

"Of course," said Morgana, "it would be foolish to just waltz in with a kitchen full of trolls."

"But aren't you worried they can smell your magic?" asked Dominic.

"There is only one troll that I am worried about, and he is over there," said Morgana pointing her Wizard Staff toward the fire.

There, Dominic saw the most enormous, fattest troll imaginable.

"He looks like a giant!" exclaimed Dominic.

The troll wore a t-shirt with a thick layer of green goop. The shirt appeared ill-fitting, straining against the bulge of his vast troll belly. He wore a chef's hat that was frayed and bedraggled, with thinning hair on his head and thick tufts between his face and chin. His skin was a sickly green, creased with wrinkles, and his teeth were yellow and prominently jutting with an overbite.

"That's the troll?" asked Dominic.

"Yes, and we need to sneak past him, or he may catch us and eat us, so we need to be as quiet as possible," said Morgana.

Morgana stealthily crept along the floor, her long wizard staff guiding her. They crouched behind a large kitchen island as the towering troll barked commands at his smaller counterparts. A sinister grin spread across his face as the minions scurried to carry out his orders.

It was a little more difficult for Barnabus to creep along quietly as his large yeti feet caused him to trip as he quietly moved around the counter. Morgana led Dominic, Leonard, and Barnabus along the rowdy kitchen, then Dominic spotted the door that swung back and forth as trolls came in and out.

"What does that door lead to?" asked Dominic.

"That leads to the dining room and our salvation," said Morgana.

She rolled over and then crept cautiously towards the door. Suddenly, there was a loud bang! Dominic noticed the enormous, unsightly troll facing away from them as they approached the door.

Dominic first noticed that the troll had stopped stirring the cauldron. "He looked around to find the noise source and saw Barnabus shamefacedly picking up his Jawa Staff. Suddenly, the troll sniffed the air.

"Sum 'in's in my kitchen."

Scurrying back and forth, the other trolls stopped, backed out of the kitchen, into the dining room, and shut the door.

"Come out, come out, dearie," said the troll.

"I won't hurt you."

Morgana shuffled to the dining room door, but the giant troll threw a big frying pan at the door, which nearly hit Morgana and blocked the door. Morgana tried using her wizard staff to lift it but was unsuccessful.

"Where are you, sweetie?" asked the troll, moving his head back and forth, searching for Morgana.

"It seems like he knows you," said Barnabus.

"Yes, we're old acquaintances," said Morgana sarcastically.

Morgana, Dominic, Barnabus, and Leonard dodged plates, spoons, and small kitchen appliances.

The giant troll ran over to them and put his hand out, ready to snatch them up, though they were still cloaked.

"Witch!" exclaimed the troll," I know you're here, and you better come out. She has been waiting for you and your friends."

Morgana strained and looked up at the troll and then at Barnabus, who was looking worriedly at Dominic, still holding Leonard.

"That's right, she knows you have friends; got yourself working for Merlin," the troll waved his hands about, still searching for them.

The troll breathed heavily.

"I can smell you and your friends but don't worry, you won't live long," said the troll.

Barnabus aimed his staff at the troll.

"That's it!" exclaimed Barnabus, "I can't take his games."

The mist cleared, and they were no longer cloaked.

"Well, well, it's been a long time," said the troll with a big belly laugh.

"You hear a lot for a creature with a big mouth," said Morgana, her wizard staff aimed at the troll's head.

The troll's giant belly shook as he made a guttural laugh.

"I hear many things in this castle, and I know who you are and which side you are on," said the troll.

"Don't think because you have your special place with the Spider Witch that you are safe," said the troll, " she is looking for you and your friends."

Morgana shot her wizard staff right above the troll's head.

"That was a warning shot," said Morgana, "the next one is free, and won't you look better as a toadstool?

"How about I serve you up into one of my favorite stews," said the troll.

The troll immediately reached forward to grab Dominic but hit hard as jets of blue light came out of Barnabus' Jawa Staff. This only stunned the troll. He shook his head in a daze, snatched all four of them up, and was ready to throw them into the large cauldron.

Barnabus tried to wriggle out of the troll's grasp, still holding his Jawa Staff, but was unsuccessful. Morgana frowned and thought she was powerful but couldn't reach for her wizard staff. Dominic, who still had Leonard, managed to wriggle free, grabbed hold of Barnabus' staff, and shot the top of the giant cauldron, quickly knocking the pot over and splashing hot liquid onto the troll's feet. The troll cried out in pain and let go of them.

Barnabus grabbed his Jawa Staff and made a troll-size prison. Barnabus, Morgana, Dominic, and Leonard rolled onto the ground out of the troll's grasp. Morgana used her staff and shot at the dining room door, and it quickly sprung open, and they dashed out towards the dining room down the hall towards more danger and ready to face the Spider Witch.

Dominic, Morgana, Barnabus, and Leonard hurried down the hall towards more danger, ready to confront the Spider Witch. All that could be heard was his hot self, heavy breathing, footfalls, and Leonard's jingling collar. Barnabus aimed his Jawa Staff at Leonard's collar to silence it.

"Hopefully, no one heard that," said Barnabus, still running.

"I am pretty sure they heard that," said Morgana, "maybe you should have thought of that before coming here."

Barnabus gave her a sideways look but didn't respond.

"Guys, maybe we should focus on which hallway to take and argue less," whispered Dominic.

Barnabus took the lead and pointed his Jawa Staff on the dark hallway, which led them to a more narrow hallway, so narrow that they could no longer travel in a group but have Barnabus lead the way, followed by Morgana, Dominic, and Leonard.

"Did I mention that I am claustrophobic," said Morgana.

"No, but this hallway is new," whispered Barnabus.

"What do you mean it's new?" asked Dominic, "that doesn't make sense; weren't you one of the king's advisors?"

Beads of sweat formed on Dominic's face. He held Leonard tightly and was drenched in sweat. He could smell a musty odor and feel large spider webs on each wall.

"Do you even know where you are going?" asked Dominic.

"Yes," said Barnabus

"How, old man?" asked Morgana.

Barnabus cleared his throat as they continued walking more slowly.

"Do you see the cobwebs?" asked Barnabus.

"Yes," said Dominic, 'but what does that have to do with anything?"

"If we are trying to get to the Spider Witch, we need to get to her first," said Barnabus.

Though he couldn't turn, he could sense their puzzled faces.

He cleared his throat once more.

"Whenever I am lost and trying to find my way around, I look for signs of where I should be going," said Barnabus.

"So, basically, we are following cobwebs," said Morgana.

"Precisely," said Barnabus.

They finally reached the end of the corridor and came to another hallway, but this time, they seemed more lost than before as there were no cobwebs to be found.

"Now, where to?" asked Morgana.

Dominic came out of the corridor and breathed heavily, thankful to be out of there. He stood on his haunches and bent over, catching his breath, as Leonard approached to lick him in the face.

" I am all right, buddy," said Dominic.

Dominic looked up to the right and pointed.

"That way!" exclaimed Dominic.

"How so?" asked Morgana.

"Because," said Dominic standing up and walking ahead of them, "Barnabus said to follow our surroundings, right."

"Yes, but why this way?" asked Morgana.

"Because it is darker this way, and if the Spider Witch is a part spider, she won't like the light very much," said Dominic.

8 MERLIN'S ARMY

Dominic led the way through the darkness. It was dusty and full of cobwebs. Dominic thought about what the Mermaid queen had given him and recalled his earlier question about the Wriggle Wraths before the mermaid had come to them as they continued down the long hallway.

"Can you tell me about the Wriggle Wraiths?" asked Dominic.

"Wriggle wraiths," Barnabus began, "come from a dark planet called Pendox. The Spider Witch comes from a distant planet very near Pendox called Gahanna. The Spider Witch sent the workers from her planet to Pendox to create a terrible creature she could use for her purpose. The Spider Witch took innocent creatures from other planets, enslaved them, broke them, and created a new species. She created a new species called wriggle wraiths to have the ability to reach into a person's thoughts and take away ideas. The wriggle wraiths only take ideas away, but the Spider Witch can reach into a mind and enslave the person. These wriggle wraiths are dangerous because they don't have their mind. They do not know right from wrong. They are created to confuse people by taking away ideas and thoughts."

So, how do we get past them?" asked Dominic, his voice trembling with fear and anticipation

"We don't," said Morgana matter-a-factly.

"I don't understand," said Dominic.

"We will help you get away from the wriggle wraiths, and you have to find the Spider Witch on your own," said Morgana.

Dominic looked at Barnabus and Morgana, confused and worried.

"Wait," said Dominic, "I thought we would face the Spider Witch together?"

Barnabus stopped walking and said, "This is your task. My job is to get you there; you must face her alone."

"So, you are going to leave me to the Spider Witch because I am somehow the only one who can face her?" asked Dominic, a mix of fear and disbelief in his voice. He clenched his fists, trying to muster the courage to confront the powerful enemy ahead, wondering if he could defeat her.

"Yes," said Barnabus sadly.

"What happened to you both being all-powerful wizards? "asked Dominic.

"We can only lead you part of the way, but you must finish the journey," said Barnabus.

"Well, that's convenient," said Dominic.

"Yes, he is good at getting you to commit to something, but you end up having to finish his work," said Morgana sarcastically.

Barnabus turned and muttered something to himself.

"What was that?" asked Morgana with a smirk.

Dominic cleared his throat, knowing full well that she was the only person capable, despite to great wizards beside him.

"Okay, we won't get anywhere by arguing," said Dominic as he sighed, "so what must I do?"

"Whatever happens, you need to do exactly as I say," said Barnabus.

Dominic smirked, trying to lighten the mood.

"Well, I managed to do one thing right.

They moved at a quicker pace now.

"And what is that," asked Morgana with a puzzled look.

"That we could signal Merlin and his army in time."

"He led them a little more sure to what looked like a hall with mirrors.

The only sound that Merlin could hear was the voices of his army. He could listen to it was the voices of his army. He could hear the clash of metal as he led his men further in and closer to the castle gates. He was covered in sweat and the muck of the earth. He looked around as he saw his men and all the good creatures of Oculus fighting alongside one another. Hours earlier, Dominic's friends, Flute and Pip, found Merlin's army. Their courage and quick thinking impressed Merlin and his generals, who appointed them leaders. Flute was tasked with leading the right flank of the centaurs, while Pip took charge of the left flank. The centaurs were the first to show the direction of the castle. Flute and Pip had earned the right to direct the cavalry of centaurs as they helped rally more who were hiding. As they led the charge, Flute, and Pip slashed right and left as they led the centaurs across the field and into the heart of the castle walls.

Merlin shot his staff straight at an ogre, who aimed his club at Flute, ready to strike, and in the nick of time, the creature missed. As Merlin got through, the gate passed the portcullis, and chaos erupted.

Arrows flew from every side. It looked like Merlin's army was trapped, but Merlin thought quickly and slammed his staff to the ground right as hands flew, and a giant blue orb of light served as a forcefield, protecting Merlin and his army.

Merlin looked around and saw a sea of arrows shooting at all corners of the castle. It was dark already, but he thought it was getting darker until he saw the arrows ricochet off his force field.

"Merlin," said Pip running towards him, "the ogres are getting ready to throw hot oil. How are we going to get out of this?"

Merlin looked around and saw his troops with a face full of fear and looked up as he saw above him threw torch light. The ogres busily made hot oil and were ready to dump over Merlin's army.

He knew then that the only way out was rallying his men and giving clear directions.

"Pip, you take your men down the left flank," said Merlin.

"Flute, you take your men on your right."

"Merlin, where do you want us to lead them?" asked Pip.

"Get them to follow your way from the castle, as we have more troops outside, "said Merlin.

"Where will you lead the middle flank?" asked Flute.

"I am needed inside of the castle," said Merlin gripping his staff harder.

Merlin gathered his staff in hand, causing the ground to shake, and a large rock emerged. Merlin stood atop the rock to address his troops. The force field buzzed loudly as everyone stood silently waiting for Merlin to give the order. Merlin's voice boomed.

"I know the enemy surrounds us, but our hearts outnumber them," said Merlin, his voice filled with passion, "we are the people of the West, the snowcapped mountains, the lush forests, the bustling capital, and the mysterious marshes. We are not just men but centaurs, fairies, elves, dryads, and metamorphagi. We represent the very heart of Oculus. United, we have the will to live, fight, and bring our beloved nation back to peace and prosperity."

"Ay!" they all shouted in roaring unison.

Merlin's men could be heard throughout the courtyard with a roar. The roar was so loud it shook the square.

"Ready!" exclaimed

"On my mark, Pip and Flute, get your men out as planned," said Merlin.

"Right!" Pip and Flute said in unison.

With a determined expression, Merlin shouted, "3, 2, 1!" He raised his staff high above his head and slammed it down against the ground with all his might.

At that moment, jets of blue light flew in all directions blinding the Spider Witch army long enough for Merlin to get to a small side door entrance and his men to escape safely.

Once the blue light dissipated, the ogres, spiders, trolls, and dark creatures looked around confusedly. One ogre suddenly pointed out towards the forest.

"Look!" the ogre shouted, "There getting' away, after them!"

The Spider Witch's army rushed, gathering clubs, mace, chains, swords, and the like to fight Merlin's army. There they quickly ran out to catch up to his men, only to be met with a larger army.

"Retreat!" one minotaur shouted with sword raised.

"Let's send these foul beasts back to the abyss where they belong!" shouted Flute as he expertly guided his centaur mount to charge against a group of menacing trolls. Elves nearby loosed arrows with pinpoint accuracy at approaching spiders, while fairies cast powerful spells to hinder the advance of the dark creatures.

"Forward!" exclaimed Pip as he approached the Spider Witch's army.

Merlin's army moved swords, stroke after stroke driving the creatures further away. Merlin's army left nearly no beast alive, and almost no trace of the foul beast, ogre, or spider was left alive. When the battle had been done, Merlin's men gave a great shout of rejoicing of freedom.

"Let's rejoice later, friends; Merlin and our friends still must end the Spider Witch's reign," said Pip.

Merlin ran up the stairs and blasted any goblin, ogre, troll, or remaining spider that came in his wake. He was covered in sweat and nearly breathless, but he could tell his apprentice needed his help. He got closer now to where he could feel Barnabus and what he feared the boy were in danger. All manner of things rushed in his mind, but he kept running down the long hallway, peering through corridors, and the like, till he came across the hall of mirrors and the putrid smell of dead wriggle wraiths.

"That's it," he thought, "I do hope the boy is all right."

9 THE SPIDER WITCH'S CASTLE

Barnabus lead Morgana, Dominic, and Leonard through a corridor with mirrors on either side. The room was dark, but Dominic could see his reflection on either side. Suddenly, a strong wind blew through the gallery. Dominic saw no wriggle wraiths, but he knew they were hiding somewhere.

At that moment, Barnabus shouted, "I can't move; it's a trap! Get out of here, boy!"

Dominic saw the hideous and terrifying wriggle wraths for the first time. As he said that, two wriggle wraiths on four legs ran out of the shadows! Wriggle Wraths have a leach's head with a dog's body. They are one of the queen's strange experiments.

"Boy, run! We will divert these creatures," shouted Barnabus. He pulled out the Jawa staff.

"I will take care of these two," said Barnabus.

"No!" shouted Dominic as he picked up Leonard.

"I can help."

"No!" shouted Barnabus.

"You need to find the Spider Witch."

The last thing Dominic saw was Morgana and Barnabus fighting together.

Barnabus' Jawa Staff was lit with blue light, and mirrors in the room blinded the wriggle wraiths as they approached Dominic. This gave Dominic and Leonard time to run out of the room.

Morgana used her staff like a sword and cut off the wriggle wrath's head. Morgana and Barnabus had both of their staff ready for another attack. Barnabus suddenly was unable to move. Morgana turned around and shot her staff off the mirror to see if any more wriggle wraths were coming toward them. Suddenly, two more wriggle wraths moved to attack with their leech mouths. Barnabus used his Jawa Staff and aimed it at the mirrors in the room. This made the most powerful light reflect off the mirror from the Jawa Staff that shot directly at the wriggle wraths. The creatures immediately hit the ground and turned to dust.

Barnabus breathed heavily and saw Morgana holding her staff and aiming at his head.

"What are you doing?" asked Barnabus, his voice shaking with betrayal.

"At last," said Morgana, her eyes cold and determined, "I can finally be free of your control."

"What?" asked Barnabus, his confusion turning to disbelief.

"What happened to working together and acceptance?" Barnabus demanded, struggling to mask the hurt in his voice.

"It was never about that," said Morgana, now circling Barnabus.

"So, you were working for the Spider Witch," said Barnabus.

"And he hits the nail on the head," said Morgana as she aimed her wizard staff toward Barnabus.

Barnabus used his staff and aimed it directly at Morgana but was blocked by her magic.

"And yet I am not working for her," said Morgana.

"So, you are a double agent?" asked Barnabus, who was now stalling and telepathically asking for help.

"But who will come and help me?" Barnabus thought to himself.

69

"Not exactly," said Morgana, "There is someone else. Someone far more powerful and showed me my full potential."

"Then why did you try and save the boy or me from the wriggle wraths or the troll?"

"I never liked that troll, and how else could I get you to trust me?" asked Morgana.

"But now, you are no use to me, and I only need to take the boy to him," said Morgana, ready to fire her staff.

Her staff started to glow dark purple when it was knocked out of her hand.

Merlin managed to free Barnabus from the ground. Now she was stuck to the floor. She and Barnabus looked at the room's entryway to see a sweaty and very angry Merlin aiming his staff at Morgana.

"Now, what are you doing?" asked Merlin, gritting his teeth.

He grabbed Morgana's wizard staff.

"I was finishing something I should have done long ago," said Morgana.

Merlin circled Morgana and nodded to Barnabus to watch over Morgana while he questioned her.

"Whom are you working for?" asked Merlin.

Morgana just smirked but did not answer. Merlin shook her, but she did not respond.

"Tell me now!" exclaimed Merlin.

"Let's just say someone older than you think, as old as time or older than you or I, as old as the Son King," said Morgana slyly.

"Who?" asked Merlin.

"You know who," said Morgana.

Merlin realized whom she was talking about and pointed his staff at her head.

"I want to know all he has planned and who else is working for him," said Merlin.

"I will only tell you a few things if you give me back my staff," said Morgana.

"Don't do it, Merlin; she is a liar," said Barnabus.

"If I give you back your staff, it is only after you tell me what he has planned," said Barnabus.

"First the staff, then the plans," said Morgana, eyeing Merlin and Barnabus.

"Fine," said Merlin.

He wrenched the wizard staff off of the floor but was stopped by Barnabus.

"This is not a good idea, Merlin," said Barnabus, "she can't be trusted; she lied to me this whole time."

"What choice do I have? You know who this boy is and what he is capable of, but if," Merlin paused, "he is back then, that is a bigger problem."

"Sometimes, you have to choose which is worse," said Merlin, eyeing Barnabus as he moved passed him.

He paused before handing the wizard staff over to Morgana.

"I will only let you out of this after we have freed the princess and you tell us what he has planned," said Merlin, "Then we will decide your fate."

Morgana raised an eyebrow but continued with her bargain.

"He is looking for the boy, and he knows exactly who the boy is," said Morgana.

"How did he get out of that place of exile?" asked Merlin.

"Oh, don't worry, he is still in exile but managed a way to send people and creatures alike to spy," said Morgana.

"He was able to persuade one advisor years ago," said Morgana.

"You remember, a Lord Destrian," said Morgana.

"Yes, I remember, and he died," said Merlin.

"Did he, or is he stuck in the place where my master resides?" asked Morgana.

"And who is your master?" asked Barnabus.

"One who is like the dark to the light," said Morgana, "One of the forgotten stories."

Barnabus was still puzzled, and Merlin looked horrified as Morgana just laughed.

"All your wisdom, and still you can't think of any great enemy of Oculus."

"I guess arrogance brings ignorance," said Morgana, "a flaw with most wizards."

"And now, let's finish this," said Morgana, raising her wizard staff as purple flames shot out of each side, aiming for Merlin and Barnabus.

An intense wizard duel erupted, with Morgana dashing between the mirrored walls, her spells casting flashes of light and color as she relentlessly targeted Merlin and Barnabus.

She quickly freed herself with her wizard staff from Merlin's binding magic. Her eyes had specks of purple flames as she missed her targets.

She moved stealthily like a cat as she gave a heavy breath and managed to aim correctly at Barnabus and get him in a purple forcefield.

Merlin dodged her magic, only to get stuck on the floor again. Morgana raised her wizard staff again at Barnabus as he could not move.

"So, you now know what it is like to be controlled, old man," said Morgana, "but unlike your ability to control with compassion, I will show mercy and end your life and take the boy to my master."

Barnabus, though unable to move, was able to speak.

"You know you don't want to hurt the boy; I saw how you grew fond of him and his dog," said Barnabus.

"Fine, you're angry at me, but leave the boy alone."

Merlin saw the conflict in her eyes and freed himself from the floor. He stealthily moved towards her and raised one hand through a giant blue orb at Morgana. She saw the orb rushing towards her and cleverly absorbed it with her wizard staff, knowing it would serve her purpose.

"Thank you, Merlin; now he has what he wanted," said Morgana.

She quickly left the room in a puff of violet smoke.

Barnabus and Merlin were left standing, both out of breath and in an attack pose.

"What was she talking about?" asked Barnabus.

"Who is this person that you put in exile?"

Merlin paused

"The Wizard Dragon, he's back," said Merlin.

"Who?" asked Barnabus.

"An old wizard," said Merlin, "Older than time. He happened to be an apprentice under the Son King but thought he could be more powerful and tried to rise but was defeated by other wizard apprentices," Merlin.

"So, you were the apprentice that helped to defeat him?" asked

Barnabus.

"Yes, but it seems he has escaped," said Merlin.

Barnabus paused and looked down sadly.

"What do you think he wants with Dominic?" asked Barnabus.

"I don't know, but one thing is for sure, we need to help Dominic," said Merlin.

With a renewed sense of urgency, Barnabus and Merlin sprinted out of the room of lost ideas, knowing they had little time to lose as they headed towards the Spider Witch's chamber to aid Dominic.

10 HOPE REKINDLED

Dominic and Leonard left the lost ideas room and ran through the castle, searching for the Spider Witch and the princess. Dominic remembered Barnabus had told him to wear a special helmet before entering the lost ideas corridor. The helmet would help keep his thoughts safe.

They soon happened upon a wall with a design. The helmets were hanging on a wall with a color pattern combination. Barnabus said he would need to find green, yellow, and red bricks in the pattern and press them three times. Dominic and Leonard stopped and looked at the colorful wall.

"Leonard," Dominic said as he searched the mosaic tile wall for the design.

"I don't see it. How will we ever find the pattern?" Just then, Barnabus ran up to them.

"What are you doing? We have to keep moving!"

"We're looking for the pattern," Dominic said.

Barnabus sighed. "There is no time for that now. We have to keep moving if we want to find the princess."

So they continued running through the castle, searching for the Spider Witch and the princess. Leonard barked aggressively at the wall near the archway. Dominic went to investigate what had caught Leonard's attention. He saw that Leonard had found a group of three bricks - one green, one yellow, and one red.

"You found it! Good boy!" said Dominic as he reached down and pressed the bricks three times in succession. The bricks moved to reveal a secret cubby containing two helmets. Dominic put one on Leonard and donned the other himself. Immediately, he could hear voices from outside the helmet, though they didn't seem to affect his thoughts. He ran through the hall until he reached the end of the long walkway, which led to a double doorway.

The gallery beyond was bejeweled with stunning gems like diamonds, rubies, and gold.

Dominic paused, took a deep breath, and said,

"I'm ready."

He searched until he found a glittering gold handle. Dominic realized that the only way he could outwit the Spider Witch was to challenge her to a battle of intelligence.

He grabbed the door handle; it made a sad singing noise as he opened it. He peered into the room and saw it dimly lit by mounted curtains on one wall. Suddenly, he saw a dark figure darting into the corner of the room. The figure moved and seemed to grow larger.

Dominic and Leonard went inside. As Dominic looked around, Leonard began sniffing aggressively, looking for any sign of the Constitution. Without warning, the figure appeared and moved toward Dominic. Its shadow was vast and dark. It had the body and head of a woman, except with spider legs. Her hair was made of writhing snakes. Leonard growled and barked as the figure disappeared.

"Ah," said the Spider Witch. "I have been waiting a long time for you."

Dominic moved forward nervously, with Leonard nearby

"You're probably wondering how I knew you were coming. Boy, I know everything. If you want to challenge me to a game of wits," the Spider

Witch snorted, "you would be foolish to do so because I will win."

Dominic became brave because he understood what Barnabus had told him when advising him in his cave. The only way to defeat the Spider Witch is by understanding her mind. He understood how to beat her by allowing her to think she would win. It was time to play a game with her, like a battle of wits!

Dominic said, " Why, majesty, we could strike a deal for whoever wins if we played a game. If I win, I take the princess, and you and your army leave this place forever. If you win, I become your slave."

"Or," the queen added, "my new statue."

"Deal," said Dominic. Leonard growled in disapproval.

"Silence that animal!" said the Spider Witch.

Dominic comforted Leonard and patted his head. "It'll be all right," he told the pup. The Spider Witch grew angry. "I'm waiting!" she said. "I am starting to feel impatient. I could forget our deal and turn you into stone right now."

"But then you couldn't test your skills and knowledge with me. Then I will know I'm more clever than you."

"You would like to think so, boy," said the Spider Witch angrily. "I'll win at this game and make you my slave."

"Shall we begin?" asked Dominic. They both sat down at a complex marble table that was slightly broken.

Dominic reached down toward his coat and held his zipper close as he watched the witch gather her thoughts.

"I see you're playing with fire, boy," she said.

"You're lucky I'm feeling merciful today."

"I see you're scared," Dominic said. "That's why you're stalling."

The witch's eyes narrowed. "I'm not scared," she said.

"I'm just trying to enjoy the moment."

"You're scared because you know you're going to lose," Dominic said.

The witch's mouth turned into a snarl.

"Fine," she said. "Let's play."

"Why have you come here, boy?" asked the spider witch.

Dominic answered with an innocent reply.

"I have come to gain back what is lost."

"And what is that?" asked the Spider Witch.

She then replied to her question. "I suppose you mean the young princess."

"You suppose?" said Dominic. "Perhaps I mean knowledge. The knowledge that was once here in Oculus, but now everything is completely dark and blank," said Dominic sadly.

"Yes, because the only thoughts people need are my thoughts," said the Spider Witch.

Dominic smirked. "Well, let's put that to the test. If you're so clever, let's see how well you do in a riddle contest."

The Spider Witch raised an eyebrow, intrigued. "Very well, boy. You go first."

"All right," Dominic said, thinking for a moment. "I speak without a mouth and hear without ears. I have nobody, but I come alive with the wind. What am I?"

The Spider Witch scoffed. "An echo. Too easy, boy. Now it's my turn. What has roots as nobody sees, is taller than trees, up, up it goes, and yet never grows?"

Dominic pondered for a moment. "A mountain," he answered confidently.

"Why would anyone want to be a free thinker?" she asked.

She was puzzled.

"Is that how your world runs things?"

"Yes!" Dominic said. "To truly have power, we first must know."

"But I have all the power," said the Spider Witch. "I don't see how your world can have more power than mine."

"Your world doesn't have light and dark, movement, or thought," said Dominic.

"It only has silence and darkness."

The Spider Witch looked disgusted. "Why would anyone want light? It hurts the eyes and burns the skin."

"Perhaps," said Dominic. "But the light brings out what was in the dark and what was lost."

As they spoke, Dominic noticed the Spider Witch had gotten closer and closer. Suddenly, she lunged for Dominic, but he unzipped his jacket and

revealed the Book of Knowledge as soon as she did, which made
The Spider Witch cried out. Her voice shook with anger. Her breath was
unsteady, and her spider legs grew wobbly, then stiff! She recoiled in horror
because she knew that this book had the power to destroy her and
everything she's built.

"Where did you get that?"

"A friend had it for safekeeping," smiled Dominic. "The Book of
Knowledge gives people the ability to think for themselves. Is that why you
can't move?"

"It's so awful," the Spider Witch whined, "put it away!"

Instead, Dominic opened the book.

The Spider Witch shrieked, and her entire body stiffened. Dominic
wondered if she was paralyzed. He could see the light peaking around the
curtains.

"Leonard," said Dominic looking at his pup, "grab the cloth covering
the window facing the Spider Witch. Hurry!"

The Spider Witch let out a scream as Leonard pulled down the curtain.
The witch's eyes darted towards another corner of the room where a cage
lay.

Inside was the princess; she was a statue. Dominic looked at the
princess's figure and saw her face freeze in a terrified expression. Dominic
turned in anger toward the Spider Witch. The Spider Witch laughed and
said,

"You will never get your princess now." At that moment, with all the
strength she could muster, the Spider Witch twitched her legs to inch
forward. Dominic backed into a large mirror in the corner as she gathered
momentum.

"Leonard, help!" shouted Dominic.

He and Leonard pushed the mirror toward the Spider Witch. When
they moved the mirror, a black hole opened in the glass! The Spider Witch
was pulled into the black hole screaming, and the book of knowledge flew
out of her hand. Pulling into the darkness, she turned back into her human
form. The book of knowledge closing itself was the last thing she saw
before the darkness consumed her.

As the mirror fell on the Spider Witch, the vortex of the black hole pulled her in. The mirror hit the floor, smashing into a thousand pieces. The black hole and the Spider Witch disappeared! At that very moment, the sun peaked through the clouds.

Dominic looked out the windows and saw that all darkness had disappeared. It wasn't just a sliver of sunlight but a brilliant and shining sun. Soon birds began to chirp. Dominic and Leonard moved to help the little princess. Dominic looked at the life-like statue of the princess. It did look just like the little princess Barnabus had described. Dominic touched the little princess's hand, and Princess Rebecca was unfrozen and awake.

"How can we, the people of Oculus, ever thank you?" asked Princess Rebecca. "You have saved me," said the princess. "You have saved us all!"

Dominic thought about it and said, "I just want to go home." Barnabus came rushing into the room, finding Princess Rebecca, Dominic, and Leonard standing together.

He looked at the princess and exclaimed, "Your majesty! I am so thankful you are safe!" Then he turned to Dominic, "Thank you! How can we ever thank you?"

Merlin and Barnabus ran into the room.

"Dominic, are you all right?" asked Barnabus.

"Yes, but the Spider Witch isn't," said Dominic.

Merlin and Barnabus looked around and saw no trace of the Spider Witch.

"Where is the Mirror?" asked Merlin.

"It disappeared along with her," said Dominic.

"We owe you everything, " said Barnabus.

"I do not think this will be the last time we see you," said Merlin.

"The only thing I want to do is go home," said Dominic.

Princess Rebecca looked heartbroken at his words, but Barnabus stepped in before she could say anything.

"I will help you get home, Dominic,"

He said, "I haven't had to use this stuff in a long time for something like this, but here goes!"

He slammed the Jawa staff to the ground, and a portal opened. Dominic looked back at Princess Rebecca one last time before saying goodbye and stepping into the portal.

"Goodbye, Princess Rebecca," he said.

"I hope to see you again soon."

Rebecca watched him disappear before turning back to Barnabus with determination.

"We will find him again," she said firmly. "My brother is out, and I will not rest until we reunite!"

"Dominic looked around and saw his clothes and shoes on the floor. The portal was gone. At that moment, his sister Rebecca walked into his room.

"There you are!" she said. "I've been looking for you everywhere."

She was about to step out of the room. Dominic said,

"Hey, Rebecca, would you like to play in my room?"

"Yes!" she exclaimed. As she pulled out a board game, Dominic thought about his adventures that day and wondered if this was the beginning of more adventures in that strange and wonderful land.

Far away in the jungle of Oculus sat a large castle. A lady appeared at the entrance of the castle gates and walked casually inside. She walked along the grand palace to a section that looked like a laboratory.

She opened the heavy wooden door by turning the knob instead of knocking.

There were all kinds of experiments going on at once. It was not a typical laboratory that a scientist might use, but it had an extensive collection of objects that looked like people but were shaped into gems of the regions they belonged to. There were beakers that you may see on one side of the wall of the room as well as a giant chess board with dragon-shaped pieces guarding something quite precious, and there in the middle of the room, sitting with a microscope in hand and a textbook to the side sat a very different person.

This person was dressed in red and black robes, similar to a kimono. He wore golden boots that looked like the armor a knight might wear. He carried a scimitar sword wrapped tight around his waist. His hair was dark as night and long but kept neat in a golden dragon clip.

He knew she was there before she even stepped into the room. His hand was raised, but without looking up, the blue magic in her staff sifted out.

He cleared his throat and looked at this powerful blue orb before placing it in a glass jar and moving toward the dragon chess piece. He didn't even look at her after putting the glass jar that held the blue orb of magic into the center of the chessboard. The dragon pieces moved closer to the glass jar and guarded it.

The man moved towards a window at the back of the room and stared out.

"It will be easy to acquire the other objects, my lord, "said Morgana.

He never acknowledged her but spoke only to himself.

"Your magic will be mine, chosen one!" said the Wizard Dragon, looking into his mirror deep in the heart of the jungle of Oculus.

Made in the USA
Middletown, DE
27 May 2023

30969046R00050